To Joey,

HAPPY HOLIDAYS

Craig O'Connor

you've gonna' love it.

HAPPY HOLIDAYS

Copyright 2009 by Craig O'Connor

Printed in the United States Of America

"This is going to be the best Christmas that this family has ever had" –

Famous Last Words

Contents

HUMBUG:
ON DISCOVERING SANTA DEAD IN YOUR CHIMNEY

Leave it to the modern-day race of ape-creatures currently in control of the calendar to get it all wrong: derived from the concept of a *holy* day and eventually morphing into the secular idea pertaining to any extra day of rest, modern man has somehow managed to turn the few holidays that occur regularly throughout the year into anything but restful. The modern American holiday is the signal for the entire family to engage in *extra* activities, to spend *extra* money, and to expend energy that they never had on normal days to make the holiday a special day, — one that will never be forgotten. It is the day in which the normal activities are suspended and different roles are acted out, all in the name of the age-old lament, "I just wanted everyone to have a nice [insert holiday here]."

There are many stories about prospective brides freaking out as their wedding day approaches as all the carefully-laid plans for the perfect wedding start to fly south for the winter. You thought PMS was bad? Just don't get too close to a bride during the hour prior the wedding rehearsal. Of course, we shouldn't laugh too hard at these crazed brides because, let's face it, as a holiday approaches and the traditions and hopes for the outcome kick in, we all become prospective brides with a forty-eight hour countdown to "I do." Factions of families that have not been on speaking terms since Truman stomped Dewey gather at the same setting, stare and grumble at each other, and start drinking. Then the homemade giblet gravy, based on a half-remembered, generations-old *separate adj.* recipe in Gallic, doesn't come out right because of a last minute realization that there's no Mustard seed anywhere within a twenty-five *lower-case* mile radius.

And the rest of the year is no different: little Jimmy's Halloween costume has turned his skin lime-green, Jennifer is allergic to her Valentine bouquet, a bottle rocket has just blown-off Grandpa Joe's left testicle in the name of Independence, an Easter Egg has gone undiscovered under the sofa until the Winter Solstice, everyone is sitting down at the table and the turkey is still trying to talk his way out of it, the dog doesn't look too good after sampling the mistletoe, the credit cards are maxed out, everyone is hung over (including the newborn if you're from an Irish family), and the holiday is ruined for everyone.

And if that's not bad enough, look at all those dishes that need to be washed!

Talk about getting it all wrong, the only holiday on which we actually take the time to rest is called *Labor Day* (that is, you rest unless you're Jerry Lewis).

Now before you start writing letters that begin with the words "Dear Mr. O'Scrooge", let me get one thing perfectly clear: I love holidays, as do all of you. If you started out as a child, chances are you have at least a few lovely memories of holidays gone by, days that were sweeter than the proverbial sugar-plum fairies doing the Cha-cha-cha. But like every other aspect of life, holidays shrink as the years go by:

what was once not just a day but a full season of joy and anticipation turns sour with the realities of life. To a child, the twenty-five days leading up to the birth of Jesus of Nazareth is filled with songs, TV specials, decorations, candy and the magical, dead-of-night arrival of a fat, jolly elf guided by a woodland critter with a shiny nose and a photographic memory of the world map. Adulthood dispels this all: the songs and TV specials become unbearable by December 13th, stringing the lights up the side of the house becomes a job (and a hazardous one at that), and the jolly old elf isn't so jolly at three in the morning when the hobbyhorse refuses to be assembled. Santa Claus is murdered by the age of ten (buried in a proper Viking funeral with an Easter Bunny at his feet), Trick-Or-Treating gives way to pitching eggs at passing cars, the Thanksgiving meal is now *your* responsibility, and Valentine's Day is not a day for the lonely. Only St. Patrick's Day gets better with age (until the doctor has a private word with you).

And yet…

There are times when, in the middle of the busiest department store, during the coldest winter, during the noisiest party, a certain feeling flashes. For just a moment, a magical warmth creeps up the spine and the soprano of our emotions hits her highest note.

And damn, can't she sing just as fine as a bluebird?

Those are the moments when we don't merely remember what it was like to be a child in the middle of a joyous holiday, but we relive it. Just for a moment.

Soon Uncle Jethro, the honorary CEO of "Bigots 'R Us", will drink four bottles of Wild Turkey and start murmuring about what the country is coming to now that one of "those people" is in the White House, but that's for later. Right now is for recapturing a marvelous moment, thought dead for many years, but now suddenly alive and smiling in your heart.

To be fair, you have to be a little bit perverse to write a collection of stories such as these, and I plead guilty as charged. For like a bride whose heel breaks on the way to the altar, nothing feels worse than when things go wrong during a meticulously-planned holiday celebration. I will never forget that sinking feeling I experienced when, stranded at JFK airport on December 23rd during a snowstorm, I pictured myself waking up on Christmas morning on the floor of the terminal. It was not a festive feeling, I can attest. When the goose ends up splattered on the floor, it hurts. When you get pulled over for going two miles over the limit in the early hours of New Year's Day, the blood-pressure soars. When every child has come home on Halloween night except for yours, the room spins.

What follows is a collection of tales of suspense and fantasy, mostly about unplanned occurrences in the midst of celebration. If nothing else, you can be thankful that, no matter how askew your holiday plans have gone, things have never gotten as bad as they have for Jake Hannay, Diane Henderson, Cletus Bruesome and the rest of the characters within.

And if things *have* gotten that bad, I suggest you put this book right back where you found it. I'm not gonna be held responsible for your flashbacks.

Let's step through the calendar, you and I, skipping the work days and ordinary weekends, to see what the holiday-makers are doing this year. You might find this enlightening, to say the least…

Happy Holidays.

Craig O'Connor
Los Angeles, CA
April 9, 2009

NEW YEAR'S DAY

MAGIC FINGERS

"Happy New Year!"

Voices rang out in Jim and Stacy's living room against the walls, just like they were likewise ringing in every home and on every TV set and on every street corner that had a person with a working mouth to shout with. Stacy passed around champagne glasses and any misgivings anyone might have had about mixing grain with grape went flying into the fireplace along with a few champagne glasses, which Jim and Stacy weren't upset about because they were made of plastic (the glasses, not Jim and Stacy). Small high-pitched horns blatted and there wasn't a single face that wasn't smiling. And all those smiles turned towards each other and eight men kissed eight women. The ninth woman, Melanie, smiled at the sheer expression of unbridled joy from everyone else at the party before needing to remind herself that she was in public and this was not the time to feel sad. Even Connie, relaxing in the arms of her boyfriend, Eric, seemed to have forgotten all the grief that drew the two women into an unbreakable friendship six months before.

Connie looked at Eric, a man who after two months had done wonders for her, and leaned her head on his chest while they both swayed gently back and forth. Choruses of "Auld Layne Syne" had broken out amongst the crowd, but Connie and Eric felt no need to join in. It was only when Connie looked to her friend that a slight trace of her once-inconsolable sadness returned. She'd asked Stacy if she could bring

Melanie along in the hopes that an evening that didn't involve pressing her fingers into wet clay might do her some good. A few months before, she herself hadn't wanted to leave the house for an evening out, but she'd forced herself into shoes and jacket and out the front door, only to find Eric at the local bowling alley. Connie had pinched herself upon returning home that night and, now that she was resting in his arms and trying to move beyond Darryl's memory, she was hoping to pass that same magic to her friend.

"Happy New Year, Melanie!" she shouted across the room. Melanie smiled, but her eyes remained vacant, her mind obviously on the little one who hadn't even made it to his first New Year's Eve.

"Group hug, Mel," Eric shouted and stretched his arms out to receive her. What a sweet guy, Connie thought, and likewise opened her arms. But Melanie didn't seem to hear them; she simply looked around herself at all the embracing couples, not seeing any of them. She took a sip of her wine and then turned and wandered towards the sliding doors leading to the patio. Connie felt a slight pang of guilt as she watched her walk out on the patio and sit down in one of the lawn chairs.

"Poor kid," said Eric, who insisted on calling Melanie a kid even though she and Connie were only two years younger than he was at thirty-one. "It must have been hard for her to come out tonight, especially since there doesn't seem to be any single guys here."

"I'm kind of surprised," said Connie. "Stacy said there might be a few turning up."

"They might, but probably not for another hour or so; they're all at other parties. She said they'll probably stagger in here when their hosts finally kick them out."

Connie shook her head. "By that time, I doubt if she'll be interested."

"Or if the guys will be able to speak coherently," Eric added. "I hate to see her so down."

Connie turned to him and put her arms around his neck. "You'd like to help her like you helped me? Not unless you have a twin brother you haven't mentioned. You're all mine!"

Eric's voice took a mock serious tone. "Aren't you being a little selfish, young lady?"

"Yep." They kissed each other lightly before Connie said, "You go have fun; I think I should talk to her for a while."

"Okay. Good luck," he said and wandered off towards the kitchen table where the snacks were. Connie took a look at the glum woman sitting on the patio and poured a second glass of wine for her. She was just about to join her when her host caught her by the arm.

"Is she alright?" asked Stacy.

"I think I know what's going through her head. Last 4th of July, I went to a friend's barbecue and I just couldn't completely join in with the fun. All I could think about was Darryl."

"Yes," Stacy said sympathetically, "Eric told me about the rough times you two have been through."

Between the day that Darryl fell fourteen stories at the construction site and the day that she met Melanie, Connie had never considered herself a lucky woman. For months, she'd wandered around the apartment that she and Darryl had shared and the park where they'd taken long, beautiful walks, wondering what she had done to deserve to have her husband taken from her. She felt like the most dejected and bankrupt person on the planet and, in her grief, could not imagine anyone suffering more than her.

Meeting Melanie changed all that. Melanie would have coped with the loss of her husband in a train wreck better if she had had her baby to be strong for. But the poor little fellow had been in his father's arms, coming back from a visit to Melanie's in-laws, when the high-speed train decided that staying on the track just wasn't exciting enough. When Melanie joined the counseling group that Connie had already belonged to for four months, the two of them found a new sister in each other. Many was the evening that Connie rocked her new friend gently as she cried into her shoulder and Connie, little by little, was beginning to find a new strength taking shape in her bones for having someone, suffering more than herself, to comfort. As far as Connie could see it, Melanie only had her and the sensation of her magic fingers in wet clay to keep herself moving from day to day.

"She seems like such a darling thing," said Stacy. "I hope she comes over more often when she's feeling better."

"Thanks; she was worried that she'd be an extra wheel around here."

"Nonsense! Everyone's welcome at the start of a new year, particularly someone who went through all the trouble to make that!"

Stacy motioned to the object standing on the coffee table that had been the topic of excited conversation through much of the evening: a two-foot high sculpture of the Baby New Year. The baby was smiling and gurgling, lying in a small field of clay daffodils and daisies, with a sash across its chest reading "2008". The work and detail that Melanie had poured into the sculpture had caused all the guests to gasp in amazement the second she arrived: the baby was lovingly painted the color of the healthiest and happiest baby in the nursery, which contrasted with the bright violet of the sash and vibrant flowers. The details were astonishing: looking closely, one could see a bee nestling in one of the flowers and a caterpillar making its way up the stem.

"My breath is taken away every time I look at it," said Stacy, in awe of the sculpture even though it had been in her home for three hours. "You've got to let me give her something for it."

"She won't take it. This is just what she does."

"Well, I wish an art dealer was on the guest list tonight; she'd be writing her own ticket. That would be a great start to the year. Just look at it: she's even put a little strawberry mark on the baby's face. Isn't it just adorable? I'm gonna keep this forever!"

Connie leaned forward and took another look at the mark, resting off to the right of center on the baby's forehead. She felt a small lurch in her throat whenever she looked at it: she'd seen a baby with that exact mark on its face before: in a picture that Melanie had shown her.

"I'm gonna go take her a drink."

"Don't let me keep you, sweetie," she said. "I know it must have been a struggle for her to come here tonight. You let her know she's welcome anytime and tell her I said 'thanks' again for the sculpture."

Connie smiled and turned back to the sliding doors separating her from Melanie. She approached it slowly, uncertain if Melanie would welcome an interruption. As she got closer, she saw that Melanie was not entirely idle.

For some reason, the grief-stricken woman had gotten a hold of a field mouse and seemed to be petting it. Connie stopped at the window and wondered what in the world had possessed her to capture a wild rodent and play with it and was glad that she was apparently the only one at the party to be witnessing it. Just as she was about to reach for the door handle, something happened that nearly made her drop both wine glasses.

Under Melanie's fingers, the mouse began to change.

She wasn't merely petting the little creature, she was firmly stroking it just behind its ear and the flesh was molding itself under her guidance. In just a few pulls, Melanie had managed to fashion what looked like a wing on the mouse's left side just behind its head.

Connie's mouth dropped open; she immediately closed it again when she thought that someone might catch her reflection in the window. She turned to look at the guests; everyone was involved in their own conversations and some had drifted downstairs to the basement, where the flatscreen TV was. Laughter and drink was keeping everyone from discovering the miracle that was currently taking place on the patio.

She turned back to find that Melanie had completed the other wing and had even managed to draw what looked like feathers with the help of a twig she'd found lying around. She then pinched the mouse's nose and drew it out to a point, creating a tiny beak, which immediately opened. Connie could not hear through the glass, but she guessed that it had just let out a tiny cheep. Melanie next smoothed down its hind legs and spindled its fore legs into skinny bird's feet. She held the creature up to her discerning eye and Connie could see that she had already fashioned tail feathers on its rear. The sculptress picked up the twig again and began scratching more feathers on its body, which had been furry before a few light strokes of her fingers did their work.

Connie drained both wine glasses and put them on the coffee table before opening the sliding door. Melanie immediately looked up at the intruder and back at the sparrow in her hand, as if checking to see if it was real-looking enough to lie about it.

"How long have you been standing there?" she asked, but Connie's silence and the look on her face told her everything. "Did anybody else see?"

Connie shook her head. Melanie breathed a sigh and loosened her grip on the bird which, to Connie's astonishment, flew up into a tree.

Melanie leaned back in her lawn chair, not saying anything or even looking at her friend, who slowly sat down on the next chair.

"How did you do that?"

Melanie looked away. "I... I don't know."

"But..." Connie searched for words as she suddenly heard the sparrow cheeping in the tree. "Have you always been able to do that?"

"No! I... I've only just recently... discovered that I could... It first happened when I was having a real bad moment two months ago. I was home alone and all the memories about Ted and Christian came back to me in a flash." She had to stop for a moment to clear her throat. "I was so angry and... I just gripped a chair for support. I clutched it so tight and worked my fingers into the wood as I thought about what happened and how unfair it all was. Then... I suddenly realized that the chair had... gone... soft beneath my fingers."

"Just like clay," said Connie.

"Yes."

"What happened next?"

Melanie looked right in her eye. "Do you remember that time you came over and remarked on that new table I had in the parlor?"

Connie nearly forgot to breathe. "You're kidding me!"

"I'm not."

"You said you paid thirty dollars for it at a yard sale!"

"Keep quiet, please!" Melanie turned to see if anyone in the house had heard them.

"Are you telling me that was once..."

"...one of the chairs from the kitchen. Remember I said that the wicker seat had given way and I had to throw it out?"

Connie just stared at the pavement, wondering if the world spinning around you on the first day of the year was a bad omen.

"At first, I tried it out on whatever I could find. I found a beer can lying on the front lawn; after an hour, I'd molded it into that vase on the kitchen table. You said a couple of weeks ago that I'd been going to a lot of yard sales lately? I haven't been to a single one in a year."

"But this just can't happen; nobody can just rub a can hard enough and…"

Melanie barely heard her and continued confessing, almost unable to stop now that what had been bottled up for so long had finally been let loose. "Then came the real test: I took a large dinner plate and started working it. I knew exactly what I wanted to make and kept it in my mind the entire time. It took hours and my fingers were nearly bleeding by the end of it, but I finally finished: I'd molded it into a record."

"I suppose next you're gonna tell me it actually played," Connie said, trying to giggle to make the reality go away. Melanie didn't laugh with her. "No… you're not saying that…"

"I knew exactly what I wanted to make and it was in my mind the whole time. Ted's favorite record was 'Abbey Road'. I haven't listened to it since the accident. I put the one I'd molded on the turntable and, from start to finish, right down to that short song right at the end…"

"But how can that be possible?" Connie was keeping her voice low, but she'd never asked a question more important in her life.

Melanie put a hand to her eyes. "I just don't know. I can only imagine that… that somehow I'm changing the very nature of whatever I start with. I've been thinking a lot about this. It's like if you see a movie with Johnny Depp and he's playing Charles Manson: he could be made up perfectly like Manson and walk and talk like Manson, but you'd know that it wasn't Manson. At the very core of his being, he's still Johnny

Depp and you're just supposed to go along with it because that can't be changed."

"But *you* can change it: you changed a mouse into a bird and it knew immediately that it could fly. How many times have you used living things?"

Melanie was almost shocked by the question. "That was the first time, I swear!"

"The sculpture that you made for tonight, what did that used to be?"

"A lump of clay," said Melanie. "As soon as I realized what I could do, I knew I couldn't do it anymore; I've been sticking with clay and paints."

"That bird didn't start off as clay. I saw it!"

Melanie's face constricted, knowing that she'd been caught. She stood up and started pacing in front of Connie, her voice choking up again. "I don't know what possessed me to do that, especially here! The question's been in the back of my head ever since I made the record: could I do it with a living thing? I didn't want to think about it. It just seemed so... monstrous. But when I came out here, I felt so sad that Ted wasn't here and... I just saw the mouse scuttling across the table and... and I just thought... 'Would he be happier if he could fly?'" She sat back down again, her head leaning far forward. "I almost don't remember doing it."

"And now you know."

"It's horrible; I'm never going to do it again."

Connie started breathing heavily. "Just one more time, please, just once for me."

Melanie lifted her tearstained eyes to look at her friend. "What?"

"I want you to make something for me."

"What could you possibly want?" she asked.

"Darryl."

There was a moment of silence between them.

"Connie, you can't be serious."

Connie gripped her shoulders. "Can't you see what you can do; what you just found out? You can change a living thing into another living thing, not just in appearance, but you can really *create* it!"

"But you can't bring Darryl back!"

"No, *you* can! Can't you see what this means to me?"

Melanie swallowed and tried to regain her composure, which was difficult with Connie staring so intently at her. "Let's just say... that I considered doing this, which I'm not. What am I supposed to use for raw materials?"

"Isn't it obvious?"

After a moment, it was. "Oh no, Connie, you can't mean..."

"I'm begging you, please..."

"But you two are so good together. I'd give anything to find a man who could make me forget Ted and Christian..."

"Do you honestly think I've forgotten him?" Connie had almost raised her voice into an insulted shout. "On nights when he can't be there, what do you think I think about, staring up at the ceiling? I've been trying to get him to move in and he wants to keep his own apartment. You know what that means; he's not sure yet! He says it's too soon and he needs his own space. How long before he gets tired and leaves me? Do you know how hard I cry in the mornings when I wake up alone? It's been over a year and it's just... *no*... *DAMNED*... *BETTER*!"

Melanie had been trying to get a word in and finally found a moment to speak. "I know what you're going through, really. But he has a family, friends... he has a life. How can you expect me to..."

But Connie fell to her knees so suddenly that Melanie looked to see if anyone in the house had noticed; they had all gravitated downstairs by this time. The woman's tears came just as quickly and her face crumbled into sorrow. "Please, Melanie, please... I need him back... you can do it... do it tonight... find somewhere quiet... think of all the times I was there for you... I was there at two in the morning once when you said you were gonna... please... do it for me..."

Connie fell forward and rested her face on Melanie's knees, weeping. Melanie began trembling, knowing that she could not possibly agree to this, but finding her will shattering. She stroked her friend's hair, being careful not to do it too strongly.

"It's like they said in group," Connie said in muffled sobs against Melanie's knees. "This is the time when we need to put ourselves first."

Melanie took only a moment more before she slowly stood up and started walking to the glass doors. "Tell him I'd like to talk to him... alone... in the car..." She sounded like a dead woman talking.

Connie suddenly jumped up. "Wait, you're gonna need

something!" She reached around her own neck and took off a locket, which Melanie took from her and opened; in the photo, Darryl had black hair as opposed to Eric's brown hair and there was a slight gap in his front teeth.

"He was five-foot-ten. Eric's only…"

"I know." She entered the house and went straight to the front door, not hearing Connie softly say "Thank you" from behind.

Eric had always liked Melanie and sympathized with her plight, so when Connie went down to the basement and whispered to him that Melanie wanted to talk to him about something out in the car, the beers that he'd drunk didn't numb his basic decency. He wobbled a bit when he stood up, but he took a deep breath, gave her a kiss, and went up the stairs to find her.

The rest of the guests were either watching the Times Square festivities or crouching on the floor shouting out disgusting trivia questions. After a while, Stacy offered to refresh everyone's drinks just as Jim's brother was trying to come up with an answer for "what famous 1930's starlet *didn't* go down on Errol Flynn". When she got to Connie, she asked, "What happened to Eric?"

"He wasn't feeling too good and decided to take a nap in the car."

"And Melanie?"

"She wasn't up to partying so she called a cab a while back."

"Oh, poor thing. Tell her we loved having her. Are you finished for the night for…"

"I'll have a large, straight scotch."

* * *

By two-thirty, most of the guests were still laughing loudly, even though Stacy was beginning to yawn. Connie had never felt more awake and alert in her life as she checked her watch for what must have been the fortieth time since she last saw Eric, reproaching herself because she had absolutely no idea how long it was supposed to take.

She did that mouse in only a few minutes, but Eric's no mouse and Darryl was no bird...

"Eric must have passed out in the car," Stacy said, still smiling with wine but with eyelids drooping.

"You know, I think I should just go out there and drive him home. Thank you so much for such a wonderful party." She stood up and touched Stacy's shoulder affectionately, hoping that she looked and sounded as if her greatest desire was not waiting for her just outside. They kissed each other on the cheek and Connie slowly retreated up the basement stairs. Once she was out of sight of the rest of the party, her walk got much faster.

Outside, she bundled against the cold air and had a bad moment when she couldn't quite remember where they had parked. Then it came to her and she scampered a short ways up the street until she saw Eric's blue Saturn sitting against the curb. The curiosity was killing her and she ran to the car and yanked the door open, sticking her head in without considering that Melanie might not be finished yet.

"How did it..." She started to ask, only to be silenced by a gentle shush. Connie looked and felt the blood drain from her head.

Melanie was sitting in the backseat, crying but with the biggest, most satisfied smile Connie had ever seen. In her arms was a sleeping baby, looking healthy, fresh and new. Melanie had never looked happier in the entire time that they'd known each other; she was the image of the Madonna on Christmas morning.

"You were right," she said, "had to do it… time to think of myself. Oh, it's alive, Connie… look at him… a New Year's Baby… just like in the sculpture. And a baby born on New Year's Day means a wonderful year ahead… you sleep now, sweetie… sleep in Mommy's arms… Mommy's got you now."

Melanie had been exact in every detail; right down to the strawberry mark just to the right of center on its forehead.

ST. VALENTINE'S DAY

FROM CUPID, WITH A VENGEANCE

Love Hurts…

That's what Gram Parsons and Emmylou Harris tell me from my IPod at least once a day, and they were right. It's never made me happy and I could never make anyone happy. They all think I'm so friendly and charming: a girl's best friend. A guy who listens and supports a woman in need gets a sweet kiss on the cheek… and that's it. And the worst thing is I treasure that moment, that tiny warm peck on my cheek that feels like an angel's blessing. I hate how goofy I feel afterwards, as if I should be grateful for getting even that thimble full of affection. I love you, Judy Price. It's real; it's true; you're the *one*! I can't live without you any longer. Please see me and love me because…

Because?

Because I want her to and that's it. Because I was getting those same feelings that I get every year when Valentine's Day starts to roll around and I know I'm going to be home watching "The Princess Bride" again, wishing that the old saying of "there's someone for everyone" wasn't a bunch of bullshit. I've listened to Judy's problems with men since she came to work at Copy Stop-ee eight months ago. I was struck by her the second she walked in to present her application: a vision of beauty with chestnut hair and a cute pair of glasses, graceful on her delicate feet and a smile that would make Jack The Ripper think twice. She likes me: she thinks I'm funny and smart and quite charming. More than once she's even said, "I don't know why you're still single. Any girl would be mad not to fall for you." All of that in the cutest English accent I've ever heard, much sexier than Keira Knightly. And I laughed, snorted an agreement and secretly screamed at the sky for her to open her eyes. The guys you go out with are all big, dumb lugs who tell dirty jokes and pinch you on the first date? How do you manage a *second* date with these flunkies? Can't you see me? Can't you hear it in my voice when I tell you that you should just forget whatever jerk you've been stepping out with because you're *better* than that? Prince Charles, Obama and McCartney combined don't deserve to rub your pretty little toes. Of course there're nice guys in America; can't you *see*?

But something stood between us, something that blocked her from seeing the real me, just like all the other girls who came before her. I never had any idea what it was; only that it was laughing at me each time my heart broke. "No, not for you," I sometimes heard it hissing in my head. "This girl is not for you. She is not the *one*. *None* of them are the one! There will never be…"

Gin helps.

On the night of February 13th, I was one of many propping up the bar at the Foxfire, where the pretty bartender thinks I'm funny, smart, quite charming and that's it. Although the martini was dry, the same was unfortunately also true for the conversation at the bar. Not a single interesting drunk had sat down to entertain me in over an hour. On a good night, a friendly gent might drink three whiskey sours and start to tell you about the White House conspiracy to beam subliminal messages of subservience into every Bluetooth on Earth (a plot that I believe I saw on an episode of *Doctor Who* a few years ago) or maybe how the Stones had put a contract out on Brian Jones so Ronnie better look out because he's next. The night just wasn't that kind of evening: on one side I had Mr. "Just-stopped-in-for-one" (boring and whipped) and on the other I had Mr. "Just-one-more-to-celebrate-something-I've-forgotten" (annoying and incoherent). Neither of them could say anything to me to get my mind off Judy and how a recent breakup with her boyfriend meant that this was going to be her first Valentine's Day in seven years without a date. Something about that annoyed me fiercely as I'd tried to sound sympathetic to her. I wanted to scream at her that seven years of dates was at least in living memory and that she should try it from my perspective.

I paid for my two drinks and slid off the stool, ready for the walk home. I stared at the floor as I went, not wanting to look at the walls. They always decorate the Foxfire when a holiday is on its way: tinsel and lights for Christmas, paper skeletons and pumpkins for Halloween, and hearts and cherubs for Valentine's. I just didn't want to look at any of them and be reminded that I not only didn't have someone to love, but also *everybody* seemingly had someone to love on Valentine's Day and that there was obviously something wrong with me for not getting with the program even *one* night a year.

Everyone's in love, I kept thinking. Even the whipped guy and the lush: they may not know it, but they have a reason to go home. Why can't they see it from *my* point of view? Why can't Judy? Why can't *anybody*?

I needed to stop in the men's room before I embarked on my twenty-minute walk. I did what I had to do, zipped up and turned towards the sink when I saw it right there in front of me: the answer to my problem.

It was sitting in a glass box attached to the wall just next to the sink. There was a tiny light inside the box shining on it and it looked like the most beautiful and the most obvious thing in the world. The manager had no doubt hung it up in the men's room as a joke, another funny tie-in with the holiday. He probably picked it up at a joke shop downtown but it didn't matter to me where he'd found it. You see, to me it was no joke. All my life I've been as nice, sweet, charming and generous as I could possibly be to every girl I'd met and none of them could see me for who I really was. I had, as of late, begun to think that I was under a curse, that maybe the face I saw in the mirror was not the face that everybody else was seeing. Was an elephant man with B.O. suddenly taking my place whenever I said "Hi" to a pretty girl?

Something beyond my comprehension was keeping Judy from seeing me: the cure was sitting in a glass box on the men's room wall.

Underneath was a sign that read, "In case of girl-trouble, BREAK GLASS!"

I broke glass.

With Judy on the rebound and all of her girlfriends going out with their men, a suggestion of Valentine's-At-An-Unattached-Friend's-Place was not a difficult thing to set up. I told her we could send out for pizza, pop a few beers, and watch *Monty Python And The Holy Grail*. Her vacant and sad eyes brightened a bit and she said, "Why not?" Not exactly "Oh, my Darling; take me by force," but at least she was coming over. And at least I got to see that beautiful smile: it kept me warm and happy all day, something that had never happened before on Valentine's Day. You see, I knew that after tonight I was going to be seeing that smile everyday for the rest of my life.

As soon as I got home I cleaned the living room and bathroom as fast and as thoroughly as I could. I got into a nice shirt, nothing too formal, and nice but relaxing slacks. The apartment smelled good, the best that it had in a long time and I felt happier than I'd ever been. This was the night my dream was finally going to come true: a lifetime of loneliness was about to be swept aside for a new, better and more fulfilling life. When I opened the kitchen cupboard to check that the thing that I'd stolen from the Foxfire was safely hidden, I had a vision of children smiling at me; not *my* children, but my *great-grandchildren*! I knew for certain whom they were and that they belonged to me: they had my eyes and Judy's smile.

Judy showed up around eight o'clock, wearing a sweatshirt, jeans and flip-flops; the polish was starting to flake off her toenails but I didn't care. She still looked gorgeous. She would've looked stunning mummified. And she didn't mind because, as usual, she didn't really see me: she didn't notice that I'd tried to look nice for the evening or that the apartment was probably cleaner than any other bachelor apartments that she might have seen in her life. She gave me a kiss on the cheek, told me how much she appreciated me inviting her over to cheer her up, and that she loved pepperoni and mushrooms. I gave her a kiss back (she turned her head before I could get to her lips) and told her to make herself comfortable while I went to find a take-out menu. As I walked into the kitchen, I mused that that was the last time she would ever turn her cheek to me.

My heart was beating heavily as I opened the cupboard and drew out the pink bow-and-arrow: the bowstring was tight and the arrowhead was heart-shaped with the bottom of the heart pointing out like a spade, very cute and very sharp. I loaded the arrow and drew it back tight; Judy's eyes had always been closed to me, but tonight they would open. It was going to work: if Cupid's Arrow didn't work, nothing would!

I stepped out of the kitchen and saw her crouching down in front of the shelves that held my DVD collection, reading the titles. She hadn't heard me: her ears were closed as well. That was about to change.

"Judy?"

She stood up and turned. Her eyes opened.

"I love you," I said gently, and fired.

The thing in my head was right: she wasn't the one.

Love hurts.

But there *is* this girl, Mindy, that I met at the Foxfire last week…

ST. PATRICK'S DAY

BLARNEYSTONED

"Are you alright to drive?"

A simple question asked with not much concern considering that the questioner, Shane's friend Mark, was at least three green pints past his normal limit and showed no signs of slowing down. But then why should he, Shane thought; he doesn't have to work tomorrow. Ah, the life of a freelance journalist must be honey in the hive, he thought. His own job at the library would be waiting for him at eight o'clock in the morning as usual and his boss wasn't the type to react favorably to any excuse that included drinking during the work week, St. Patrick's Day or not. Mark had just asked the question because that's what you did when you went out drinking with friends and Shane, who felt fine and was worried that Mark might actually offer to drive him home, responded honestly.

"I'm fine. I'll be alright. I'll call you tomorrow." Now, Shane was asking himself the same question.

Am I alright to drive?

It was a pointless question to ask considering that he'd been on the road for ten minutes. Still, it was better to ask the question ten minutes too late than to not ask it at all, so Shane took a moment to mentally check himself out as the car cruised down the boulevard.

"Okay, eyes a bit tired," he mumbled, "head not tired but slightly jumbled, stomach full of green beer and bladder filling up. I know what direction I'm going in, what street I'm on and how fast I'm going, which is forty. Bit fast, but there are no other cars around. In six minutes I'll be home, in eight I'll be in bed and everything is perfectly..."

There was a thud and the car jolted as it hit something on the side of the road, where it had been drifting to. Shane hit the brakes immediately before he realized what was happening. He was unprepared for the forward momentum that hurled him towards the windshield and felt the seatbelt strangling his chest and left shoulder. The rear of the car felt like it might swerve forward into the street. He gritted his teeth and said a quick prayer.

A moment later, Shane fell back into his seat as the car came to a rest. His hands started to tremble on the wheel and his shoulders and head soon followed.

Oh my God; what did I just hit? Let it be just a skunk.

His hands continued to grip the wheel, not wanting to begin taking the necessary steps to investigate what had been on the side of the road. Shane just sat there breathing, knowing that he had to get out of the car and toying with the idea of just putting the car in gear again and slowly driving away.

There's nobody around: no cops, no other cars, all the lights are off in the houses, maybe nobody heard me...

Shane shut the engine off. Slowly, he grappled with the seat belt to unlock it, turned on his hazards and opened the door. Stepping outside, he took what he believed would be the longest walk of his entire life, five steps, until he could see the body lying in the grass against the fence surrounding a darkened house. He could just make out a few details from a streetlamp further down the street.

The body could not have been more than four feet tall.

"Oh dear Jesus," he gasped.

A child! A child wandering around in the middle of the night! It's not moving... and the blood...

Blood had spattered along the side of the road and against the white wooden fence. It would have to be white, he thought; everyone will see that. Dizziness swept over Shane that had nothing to do with the beer he'd drunk and he stumbled closer to the body, nearly losing the strength in his legs and falling along the way. He had the presence of mind to sidestep the blood and gingerly walked through the small stretch of grass until he was standing over the small corpse. No cars drove by and no windows went up.

It doesn't matter if anyone sees me; there's no way I'm gonna walk away from this. A child: it had to be a child. Maybe I'll get lucky and God will strike me dead right here and they'll find us together at sunrise.

Shane gripped the fence and tried to lean as close to the body as he could to see if he could hear any breathing. He couldn't. With hands shaking even worse than before, he felt along the neck to see if he could detect a pulse. There was none, but what he did feel made him gasp.

This kid has a beard!

Shane took a deep breath, clutched one of the shoulders and rolled the body over, immediately wishing that he hadn't. The chest and stomach had been torn open and the flesh flapped in two different directions, exposing the ribcage. The torn stomach fell out of the body and plopped on the ground in a puddle of bile.

Shane shut his eyes tightly and shook his head, trying to drive the image away. For a moment, he thought his five green pints were going to come back up again and he fought his nausea, knowing no pit of Hell would be too horrible for a man who not only killed a person in a drunken accident but had puked on the corpse as well. He lifted his head and took deep breaths of the cold night air. When the sickness passed, he opened his eyes and forced himself to look at the corpse's face.

The small man indeed had a beard, gray with bits of red in it, quite long and thick. His gray hair was long and would have hung down past his shoulders if he had been standing, though the top of his head was bald. The face was contorted in pain; the man had obviously not known what had killed him, only that he was dead. The man's nose was quite bulbous and his whole face was lined and cragged, except for his cheeks which were rounded and probably looked quite cheerful when he smiled, not that Shane would see him smiling anytime soon.

A dwarf: an elderly dwarf...

Shane was momentarily relived to discover that it had not been a child who had been crushed by his front right bumper, but dead was dead and a dead old man was hardly better, particularly if that man was a dwarf.

Overcome with the reality of what he had done, Shane felt tears welling up in his eyes and a moan escaped out of him. He immediately covered his mouth, not wanting to make any more noise that would alert strangers. With his mouth clasped shut, Shane moaned harder and stepped backwards away from the dead man. Then he tripped on something that was lying on the ground and fell against the fence. He didn't hit the ground, but he held his position for a moment to see if he could hear anyone approaching. The street and surrounding houses were still empty. He looked at his watch and found it was nearly 1:30. It seemed impossible that no one had heard, come to investigate or even driven by since the accident, but he didn't begrudge what little luck he had. He reached down into the darkness and found what he had tripped over.

Shane was holding a thick, crooked, sturdy stick made of what looked like strong oak, blackened from heat. It felt heavier than it looked and he realized that the knob at the top had been artificially weighted, and he slapped it into his palm several times to test its strength. Given what day it was, the words "cane" or "walking stick" did not enter his head as quickly as...

"A shillelagh."

Shane forced himself to look at the little man and, ignoring the damage that his car had done to him, he noticed for the first time that the man was dressed in an old-fashioned square-cut coat laced with gold and lined with buttons that would have been shiny had they not been covered with blood. His shiny shoes, nearly free of gore, had buckles on top. As he moved forward, Shane felt his foot kick something and, reaching down to investigate, he plucked up a small, cocked hat.

He must have been coming home from a party, he thought; a St. Patrick's Day costume party. He was dressed as a leprechaun. Look at that; he put a hell of a lot of work into that costume. He looks just like a...

And then Shane's eye caught something that was lying on the ground about ten feet from the little man's foot: a small mound of cloth caught in the dim light of the distant street lamp.

Shane hurried to the spot where the parcel lay and found that it was a cloth, draw-string purse, slightly bigger than his own hand. He picked it up and was amazed by how heavy it was. Jingles came from inside.

"Part of his costume," he muttered. "Leprechauns always have money on them. Oh, the poor little guy..."

Shane opened the purse and was shocked to discover, instead of pocket change, gold coins jangling in his hand. Part of his mind tried to convince him that it was just an elaborate prop to complete the little man's costume; they had to be painted plastic or wrapped chocolate, but his hands told him differently. He pulled one out and looked at it the best he could in the dim light.

The coin was unmarked, just a small disk of dirty-yellow metal, grubby from unclean fingers rubbing it incessantly. He hefted it in his hand and found it had the right weight. He tried bending the coin and found it malleable. Despite all the sensible things he was trying to tell himself, the coin was gold. And despite all the sensible things he was trying to tell himself, the little man with the beard, square-cut coat, buckle shoes, cocked hat, shillelagh, and purse of gold coins was a...

"It can't be," he said.

He hefted the bag again; there were quite a few coins in his hand. There was also a small corpse lying on the side of the road that would not go undiscovered forever.

Who's ever going to believe that I just ran over a real Leprechaun? They'd lock me up as a loony.

What else was there to do?

* * *

Shane took a long hot shower when he got home and somehow still managed to have a few traces of blood under his fingernails. He was horrified and scrubbed his fingers in the sink furiously until his fingers were red from rubbing. After making sure his hands were clean, he still felt panicked, his mind unable to stop picturing the little man and his possessions just before he closed the trunk on him. More than anything, he wanted and needed a drink and he was not going to deny himself despite how much he'd had at the Irish pub. He never felt more sober in his life and he became afraid that the walls of his mind would crumble completely if he didn't get a drink into him immediately. He went straight from the bathroom, naked, to the cupboard where he kept the alcohol. He chose at random, but wasn't surprised to find the whiskey bottle in his hand. With his head splitting, he forgot to get a glass, ice and a little water and simply put the bottle to his mouth and took three big swallows. He nearly choked on the second as his throat struggled against the liquid fire, but he forced a third swallow down anyway. He nearly dropped the bottle as he let the stuff work its magic on his stomach and brain and he groaned in satisfaction.

He nearly put the bottle back when his eye caught a glimpse of the coin purse, full of treasure, sitting on the kitchen table: it was the only one of the little man's possessions that he hadn't left in the trunk.

"Time for a decent one," he said as he reached for a glass and then went to the freezer for the ice.

Twenty minutes later, after a few "decent ones", Shane staggered into his bedroom, the three-quarters empty bottle still in his hand and slumped down on the bed, not bothering to find his pajamas or get under the covers. He lay there with his pimpled ass facing the ceiling, gurgling and muttering as he waited for sleep or a blackout to take him, either one was equally welcome.

Words whispered out with every breath. "I'll call Felson tomorrow… too sick to work… let the asshole fire me… I've got some money… wash the car tomorrow… get that thing out of there… there are no leprechauns… can't kill what doesn't exist… no laws broken… didn't do anything wrong… accident… no leprechauns…"

Tap-tap…

One eye opened. Shane wished he was drunk enough to pretend that he hadn't heard it. He vaguely thought that the sound had been a dream, something that would be punishing his sleep for nights to come. He started to close his eye again.

Tap-tap-tap…

Both eyes opened and Shane groggily pushed himself up, trying to focus his vision on the far window. In his rush to collapse into bed, he'd forgotten to close the blinds, and the street lamp outside was illuminating a small head on which sat a cocked hat.

Tap-tap-tap…

A crooked knob-handled stick, like the little man's shillelagh was tapping lightly on the window. Shane cursed to think that the little man's small but strong club, locked with his corpse in the trunk, wasn't within arm's reach at that moment.

I'm not seeing that. I'm not hearing that. I'm on the second floor; a grown man couldn't reach up this high, let alone a… there are no lepre…

The shillelagh drew back and smashed out the glass in a single swipe. Shane leapt back to the headboard as the shattered glass flew inward. His reflexes fought against his inebriation as he pressed himself against the wall, staring at the figure rising up and climbing through the broken window. Despite what must have been a tough climb up the side of the house, his coat was immaculate: dark red in the sparse light, and the seven buttons lining it glinted when he shook himself to unloose the fleas from his long beard. The buckled shoes crackled on the broken glass and the look on his face was wild with rage.

"Is dis how y' dress fur cump'ny, laddie?" he asked with scorn. Shane remembered that he was naked and placed a hand between his legs, wincing as his fear caused him to squeeze. He was trying to think of something to say when another little head, breathing heavily, appeared at the broken window. The second figure hurled himself in with a mighty grunt and was standing next to his friend in a moment.

"Is he t' one, Redmond?" he asked the little man who came in first.

"T' one that murdered 'r Seamus fur his gold? He be t' one," Redmond said as more little men climbed up through the window and stood in a tight crowd behind their leader, each one carrying a cudgel. "He went a-hunting tonight. Went a-hunting fur gold, dis one did. Found it, too. Lucky lad; all he had t' do t' get his hands 'n t'was t' crush 'r Seamus beneath his 'sheen."

The twelve men facing Shane all murmured in grumbling agreement.

"I seen i t'appen, crush'd 'im wit' no second t'ought!" said the last one to come in as he charged to the front of the pack and pointed his finger. "Went straight fur t' purse, he did! 'N spat upon 'r Seamus as well!"

Shane finally found his voice. "It was an accident," he said hoarsely. The twelve men grumbled.

"Y' heard dat, brothers?" asked another. "He stole t' purse by accident!"

"No," pleaded Shane. "You don't understand!" But the one that claimed to have seen the accident continued.

"Den he labored t' steal 'r Seamus's body, locked 'im in his 'sheen! No proper wake fur t' eldest son of 'r clan!"

"Did anyone else see wha t'e done, Snuffy?" asked another of the pack of the one witness.

"Nay, I made shoor o' dat," said Snuffy. "Spake charms, invok'd 'cantations, kep folks away."

Shane felt his stomach sink inside him; these men had saved him for themselves, for this moment. Through all the grumbling and the accusations, Redmond remained quiet, his mean eyes fixed on the naked man. Shane couldn't help but focus on the silent, stewing dwarf.

No, not a dwarf… a leprechaun… twelve leprechauns…

Redmond took a step forward and the rest of the pack followed him. "Lad went a-hunting fur gold 'nd found it." His voice suddenly dropped, although Shane could still hear him. "Y' daren't go a-hunting…"

The words came out of Shane's mouth unconsciously. "…for fear of little men."

With a collective roar, twelve cudgels rose up in the air.

Shane tried to run for the door, but the mattress betrayed him and he took an awkward bounce and landed off balance. The head of Redmond's shillelagh smashed into Shane's naked knee and he howled, realizing the heads of the clubs had been filled with lead to make them heavier. He went down, trying to keep one hand between his legs and the other frantically waving off the mass of clubs that were beating down on him. His ribs, ass, knees, shoulders and feet all sustained an onslaught of mighty blows from the little men, whose voices all raised up in a jumble of fierce hatred and revenge. Shane looked up to see the rage in Snuffy's eyes just as his club flew into his face.

* * *

"What should we do w' tim?"

"Y' know what I tink."

Shane awoke on the floor of his bedroom with his body aching all over. He could feel shards of broken glass beneath him. He tried to bite back a moan, but the pain was too strong.

"Wakin' up, brothers."

"So what? We got 'im."

Shane didn't want to open his eyes but his curiosity got the best of him. The twelve men were standing in a huddle, the closest one within arm's reach, but Shane did not dare to try to go for him. Standing would not be a good idea considering what they'd already done to him. He was reasonably certain that nothing was broken and he tried lifting his arm. He moaned miserably.

The closest one turned around and gave him a swat on the shoulder with his club. Shane howled.

"Shut y' mouth," said the little man, giving him another swat. "We c'nt hear 'rselves tink!"

Shane sank back to the floor and tried to be as quiet as possible. After another minute of murmured discussion, the voice of Redmond rang out.

"So, we're agreed?"

The eleven others shouted a raucous affirmation. As one, they all turned on Shane, who started to rise from the floor as they stepped towards him.

"What are you doing?"

"Y' like gold," said Redmond. "We'd not dis'point y' after t' work y' dun. So, we'll give y' as much gold as y' want."

Shane was fully up on his feet, aching all over from the beating and from stepping on the broken glass.

"I don't want your gold."

"But y' kill't 'r Seamus fur't."

"That was an accident, I told you!" Shane felt the corner of the room at his back.

"We've heard 'nuff o' dat." Redmond then shouted, "Brothers!"

The twelve little men began chanting as one, their voices gently lilting into Shane's ears. He started feeling sleepy and, although he would not fall, his legs didn't want to move from their spot. He held out his hand.

"Stop it! Whatever you're doing, just stop it!"

The last thing he saw was Snuffy pulling a sack out of his coat, reaching in and throwing a large handful of powder in his face.

* * *

In the early morning of March the 18th, before the sun had risen, a group of twelve little men trudged through the woods that led back to the cave that they called home, a cave that no human could or would ever stumble upon in a million years, hidden as it was by the magic sapling of blackthorn that stood in front of it and made it invisible to human eyes. They began whistling "Galway Bay" when they had reached the point in the woods where they were sure that no one would hear them. Despite their short stature, their combined strength was enough to carry their prize back to their lair, and they did so without protest or grumble. It had been tough, losing old Seamus like that, but what they got in return more than made up for it.

Redmond led the way and, as he got to the blackthorn sapling, he stood aside and allowed the rest of the pack to pass him while he looked up and marveled at their prize for the evening: a golden statue of a naked man with one hand reaching out in terror.

APRIL FOOL'S DAY

WHEN EDDIE DISAPPEARED

When Eddie Nightingale, ten years old, disappeared on April 1st, 1976, everyone thought it was a joke, considering what day it was and what Eddie was like. Eddie Nightingale was *that* kid in the neighborhood that comes along every ten years or so. Every neighborhood has one: the one with the laugh that isn't really a laugh at all but a rebel yell that signaled to all within earshot that something that was definitely *not* funny, something that *he* had caused more often than not, had just happened. The laugh was often heard when a younger child was knocked off a bicycle, when a bird fell dead from a slingshot projectile, and when old Mrs. Bainbridge stepped in a puddle on her doorstep that most definitely wasn't water. Oddly, there was no meanness in his face at all; he either hid it well or simply didn't understand the consequences of his actions. These were the things that made him happy, made him joyful, filled him full of spunk and energy and gave him a reason to spring out of bed in the morning with a love of life that matched no other person on the planet. The smaller kids feared and avoided him while the older kids admired how he kept coming back to play tricks on them no matter how many times they beat him up. The grown-ups, who grew tired of phoning Eddie's long-suffering mother about his latest offense, just wished he would disappear, which is exactly what he did.

That year, April 1st fell on a Saturday, Eddie's favorite day of the week, although he had been a bit disappointed to discover that he could not enjoy April Fools Day amongst the kids and teachers of Carter Elementary School (where the blast of a cherry bomb always rang majestically in the acoustically-perfect boys' room). Still, Eddie being Eddie, he decided to take that particular lemon and make piss-flavored lemonade (not literally, of course, as that had been last year's major attraction and hadn't Mom been mad about *that* one). There were plenty of chances for fun in the neighborhood and, if he just thought ahead just a bit, Mom would never need to know. So during the week that led up to April 1st, Eddie was quieter than usual, which made his mother and eight year-old sister Sally nervous.

On April 1st, Eddie woke up very early, just at the first smattering of sunrise, and snuck out of the house before either his mother or Sally had even begun to stir from slumber. When they awoke, they ate their breakfast and Mrs. Nightingale tried to keep her mind from wondering what her rambunctious son, whom she loved very much (she told herself), was up to. Sally had once asked, not too long before, why Eddie was so mean to everybody and her mother, who truly took each act of mischief to heart and disciplined her son the best she could without doing anything that would arouse a social worker's interest, was genuinely taken aback. While part of her mind wondered the same thing, she spoke her heart to her daughter.

"Honey," she'd said, "your brother isn't *mean*! I know he does a lot of things that bothers the other children, but he just doesn't understand…" And then her voice had trailed off. *Why* didn't he understand? Hadn't she told him time and again, yelled it over and over until his smile finally began to fall and he seemed to get it, that what he was doing just wasn't *nice*? Wasn't the beatings that the older kids gave him whenever he messed with them evidence enough? Did he not understand that every action has a consequence?

He just doesn't understand... when he gets beaten up or when I yell at him and take away his TV privileges, he's hurt and gets upset... but he doesn't learn... he doesn't see the reasons why... he'd trip an old woman and then wonder why she hit him with her cane... he doesn't see it...

Well, there *was* that one time, she thought. A year before when he'd pushed Sally down the stairs and dislocated her shoulder. Mrs. Nightingale made sure – damned sure – that Eddie realized and understood that what he'd done was wrong and that he'd better never, *never*, do anything to his sister again. Eddie had trouble sitting for a few days afterwards, but the result was real: he steered clear of Sally from that point onward.

The phone rang at about 10:30 that morning, not long after Sally got dressed and went out to play. Mrs. Nightingale's hand faltered on the way to the receiver and she took a deep breath before answering.

"Hello?"

There was a sigh on the other end before the voice finally spoke. "Your son... do you know what he's done?"

Someday, I'm going to write a book with that title.

"Hello Janet, what's he done, now?"

"My flowers..."

"He trampled them?" Mrs. Nightingale asked, not really believing that Eddie would go for something so simple. "Did he dig them up?"

"You're not going to believe this, but he picked all but a few of them and the ones he left behind form letters that I can see from my bedroom window! *Four* letters! Guess what the first letter is?"

Mrs. Nightingale closed her eyes, feeling the beginning of a really grand headache festering just behind her eyes. "I think that he might have spelled a word that the principal told me Eddie has recently become fascinated with at school."

"Yes, I know they all go through that phase. They love saying it when there are no adults around, but I don't know of any of them that spell it out in flowers! Really, you've got to do something about..."

Mrs. Nightingale gave her usual response, that she would certainly punish Eddie for this latest offense and promised to make restitution if it was required. She hung up the phone, slipped into a pair of tattered flats and went into the neighborhood to put an end to her son's tirade before it could get too far out of control.

She walked down the street, where neighborhood children were playing stickball or riding bikes, activities that bored Eddie quickly, unless the stick could be used to swack another boy on the butt when he was least expecting it or the bike could be charged at a group of girls playing hopscotch. Mrs. Nightingale hated herself when her mind instinctively pondered about what kind of trouble her only son could be creating, but there was little that she could do to stop it: experience had taught her to always be on her guard where her son was concerned. She loved him dearly, would've torn down the walls separating this world from the next to protect him, but in her darkest moments, when the phone would ring yet one more time or when that horrible laugh of his would ring through the neighborhood, Mrs. Nightingale silently and secretly wished, just for a few moments, that her son would just simply…

Her ears picked up a sound just above the normal din of playing children: further away, a few blocks at least, a little girl breathlessly crying and calling "Mommy". Mrs. Nightingale stopped and felt her stomach lurch; it was the same exact cry that she'd heard a year before when Sally broke her arm… when Eddie had pushed her…

Sally!

Mrs. Nightingale turned to her right at the corner where Nye Avenue and Garden Road met and could see Sally running down the middle of the tree-shadowed street. Immediately, Mrs. Nightingale was struck by the sight of her daughter, who always stayed on the sidewalk even on a street like Garden Road where there were hardly ever any cars, running and crying as if she'd lost all sense of direction and reason. She took two steps towards her daughter and then nearly stumbled as she finally got a good look at the girl as she emerged from the shadows: her face and the upper part of her T-shirt were covered in red.

Blood!

"Mommy," Sally screamed as she ran down the street. Other children playing on Nye had heard Sally's cries and started drifting away from their games to investigate. Mrs. Nightingale regained her feet and ran towards her daughter, whom she could see was running with her eyes squeezed shut.

"Sally," Mrs. Nightingale called, "I'm right here! Are you alright?"

Sally, who had been running diagonally across the length of the street, turned slightly to her right at the sound of her mother's voice, slipped when her foot came down on some leaves and landed sprawled on the pavement, crying the whole time.

Mrs. Nightingale reached the girl in a matter of seconds and scooped her into her arms, feeling the stickiness on her. At her first hysterical glance, she hallucinated a large, gaping wound in Sally's neck, spurting her lifeblood all over her clothes and onto the street. After a minute, she realized that her daughter, save for a scrape on her nose and forehead from the fall, was whole and a familiar smell came to her.

"It's paint," she said to herself. "Red paint." Sally pressed against her and wept into her shoulder while she comforted the girl. She became aware of the children from the other street creeping closer and the whispers behind her.

"Look, is she bleeding?"

"They both are, look…"

"Ga-ross! What happened to them?"

Then there were sounds of doors opening and windows going up. Someone from one of the houses shouted, "Do you need help? Shall I call an ambulance?"

She hugged Sally tighter to her and stood up. "No, it's just red paint. Somebody…"

You know who…

"...splattered her with red paint. She's not hurt." Then she spun around to the other eyes and faces surrounding her and said the same thing. "We're alright, I promise! It's just paint! You can go now!"

The excited looks on the other children fell as they could see for themselves the truth; the little girl and her mother were too bright red to really be covered in blood. It *had* to be paint and Mrs. Nightingale was surprised to hear disappointed groans from the kids as they trudged back to their games, now that the most exciting thing to happen in the neighborhood for years turned out to be some cry-baby girl and her hysterical mother. As they were left alone, Mrs. Nightingale felt her daughter crying and coughing snot into her shoulder.

"It's okay, Honey, it's okay," she whispered. "Did you hurt yourself when you fell?"

Sally didn't answer at first, her sobs too big to allow words out. When she finally brought her head up and looked into her mother's face, her own face splattered fire-engine red, she said, "Why, Mommy? Why does he have to be so *meeeean*?"

If she had said that about her father, she thought, I would've gotten a divorce and a restraining order. But Eddie...

And then a realization swept over her.

I'll kill him for this.

"What happened, Sally?"

Sally hiccupped. "I was riding my bike on the sidewalk and I heard him yelling from behind Mr. Myers' house. He was calling for help really loud. I thought he got hurt or something. So I put my bike against a tree and ran around to Mr. Myers' backyard. And there was

nobody there at first and then he jumped out from behind a tree and…"
Sally started to cry again, but her mother encouraged her to continue.
"…he yelled 'April Fools' and threw a water-balloon at me and it was
full of paint and I couldn't see and… Mommy, he's just so *meeeeeean*!"

"Oh sweetie," said Mrs. Nightingale and hugged her daughter
tight to her chest as she got her last few sobs out. "I know he scared you,
but you're alright. Don't cry. Take a deep breath. Feel better?"

"Uh-huh."

"Good. Now, come with me. Mommy's going to straighten this
out."

Mrs. Nightingale put Sally down on her feet, took her crimson
hand and walked the painted child down the street to the Myers' house.
The chances were good that Eddie was still there in Mr. Myers'
backyard, lying on his back, kicking his legs up and laughing up a storm.
Since he never considered his actions to be anything but one colossal
joke, it often never occurred to him to run and hide once his dirty work
was completed and Mrs. Nightingale could picture him there right at that
moment, holding his stomach as the laughter poured out of him and no
doubt happy to be alive. As they got closer, Mrs. Nightingale felt her
feet fall into a quick march, as if she were advancing across the
battleground for the final charge. This time there would be no letting up;
there would be no third chances, and definitely no mercy. The thought of
what the neighbors would think about what she was going to do never
entered her head. Only one thought kept her moving as she marched
around the side of Mr. Myers' house: she was going to make Eddie eat
his laugh once and for all.

Mother and daughter, hand in hand, came round the side of the house and entered Mr. Myers' backyard. The first few specks of red paint on the grass that Mrs. Nightingale caught sight of brought her temper to the breaking point and she screamed at the person crouched down with his back towards her.

"EDDIE!"

The crouched figured turned sharply and Mrs. Nightingale was staring into the frightened and confused face of Mr. Myers, dressed only in jeans and a wife-beater undershirt. He cowered back slightly, as if guilty at being caught red-handed at something. All around him, the grass was splattered with the same red paint that covered Sally.

Mr. Myers' jaw quivered as he tried to find words. Finally, he jabbered, "I didn't do anything!"

Something inside Mrs. Nightingale fell with dizzying swiftness. This was not what she was expecting to hear from a man in his own backyard. There was a sharp smell that made her cough slightly.

Didn't do anything? Who said he did anything? What the Hell is he doing out here, crawling around in his bare feet?

It was Sally who swallowed her last sob and found the voice to speak. "Mr. Myers, did you see my brother down here? He threw a paint balloon at me. Did you see where he went?"

Mr. Myers rolled off his knees and sat down, cross-legged, on the grass, still looking totally lost as to where he was. He looked down and started pulling at the grass.

Mrs. Nightingale finally spoke up. "Ben, did you see where Eddie went? As you can see, he made a mess of both your lawn and Sally. As soon as I find him, I'll teach him a lesson that he'll never…"

"I heard him down here," Mr. Myers said, quietly as if talking to himself. "I was taking a nap and I heard him shouting for help. I was really sleeping and it took me a few minutes to finally wake up and realize that someone was down in the yard. I went as quickly as I could to the window. I saw him hit your daughter with the balloon. She screamed and cried and all he did was laugh at her. It sounded just like my older brother when I was a kid and he used to play mean tricks on me; really cruel and vengeful, you know?"

Mr. Myers simply looked at Mrs. Nightingale and lapsed into silence, as if hoping for an explanation for the existence of her hell-raising child. She didn't know what to say and wondered why he was acting so strange. More and more, she began to suspect that something terrible had happened.

"Ben, what happened?"

"I stuck my head out the window and told him to get the hell out of my yard," he answered, still drained of emotion. "Then the little shit stuck his middle finger up at me. Sorry, honey."

This last he said to Sally, who gasped at the sound of the word that her mother had warned both her and Eddie never to say, although Eddie had said it plenty of times when her mother was out of earshot. Mrs. Nightingale patted her daughter's head and nearly missed what Mr. Myers said next.

"Then he disappeared."

"Yeah, Eddie's fast when he wants to make a getaway. Do you know which way he went?"

Mr. Myers stared at her and his eyebrows furrowed. "Didn't you hear what I said? He disappeared!"

"I heard you, Ben. Just tell me which way he went and..."

"He didn't go any way! He didn't move from this spot! I'm telling you, he vanished! Your son literally DISAPPEARED FROM THIS SPOT!"

Part of Mrs. Nightingale believed the shocked man immediately, but there was nothing in her experience to deal with such a turn of events, so she fell back on doubt. "Ben, stop saying that."

"I saw it! It happened right in front of me!"

"You must've turned away or blinked or something. You'd just woken up; isn't it possible that maybe you just..."

"That kid disappeared, right where he was standing. When he flipped me the bird, I yelled that I was coming down and he just smiled this big grin, laughed a couple of times, and then he vanished. It took him right in the middle of a laugh and there was like... this echo... like he fell down a hole or something. It was the damnedest thing I ever saw! I ran right down here to see it for myself and when I got down here... it was like... I could smell something like... electricity."

"Don't be silly," said Mrs. Nightingale.

"DO I LOOK LIKE I'M BEING SILLY?"

Sally cowered against her mother's leg and started crying again. Her mother picked her up and hugged her. "Ben, you're scaring her!

I don't know what you were sleeping off when the children woke you, but I don't appreciate you carrying on like this!"

"The smell's still here," he said, his voice choking. "Can't you smell it?"

Mrs. Nightingale took a strong sniff and felt a sharp tingle strike the back of her nose. It was like that whiff in the air when something electrical in the house blows, like a fuse or a Christmas light. She held a finger to her nose to keep from sneezing.

Mr. Myers was breathing heavily as he continued. "I had to see if there were any traces, anything that might tell me what happened to him. I came down as quick as I could and I was looking where he was standing when he dis…"

"Stop saying that!" Mrs. Nightingale squeezed her daughter tighter as she shouted.

"Mommy, you're hurting me."

Mr. Myers ignored them both as he stretched his arm behind him and pointed. "There, it was right there. Can you see what's there?"

Mrs. Nightingale stepped forward, with her daughter in her arms, and carefully stepped past the shaken, obviously hung-over man in his undershirt and looked to where he was pointing. There in the grass, just shy of the shadow of the trees, were two charred sneaker prints.

"Mommy, you're hurting me again."

Mrs. Nightingale knew she was, but she couldn't help but hug her daughter...

(your last remaining child)

(STOP THAT!)

...tighter to her. Her entire body began to shake and she bit the inside of her cheek to bring herself back from the point of collapsing to the ground with Sally in her arms. She turned away and was surprised to find that Mr. Myers had gotten up and was heading for his back door without her hearing him.

"Ben, where are you going?"

Without turning back, he said, "I'm going to call the police."

"And tell them what?"

With one hand on the doorknob, he turned back and answered her. "I'm gonna tell them what I saw and I don't care if they think I'm nuts. At least it'll be on the record that I called the police, so they won't think I had anything to do with it!" He was inside the house before Mrs. Nightingale could say anything else.

Mrs. Nightingale stood in Mr. Myers' backyard with Sally in her arms, hardly breathing, trying to get her mind around the last few minutes. Very quietly, Sally said in her ear, "He was right there."

"What, Honey?"

"Eddie was standing right there when he threw the balloon at me. Right where it's all black."

"Don't look at it. We're going home."

"But Mr. Myers said…"

"Forget about Mr. Myers. He was drinking last night and he was confused when Eddie woke him up. He doesn't know what he's talking about."

"But…"

"No buts! We have to get you cleaned up. What kind of mother am I to let you walk around covered in paint? We'll go home, get you cleaned up, I'll make you lunch and then I'll go looking for your brother. And when I find him…"

Sally struggled in her mother's arms. "Mr. Myers said that Eddie…"

"Hush," she said more forcibly than she wanted, but she was afraid that her head was going to explode from the dreadful pounding if she heard that lie one more time. Hugging Sally tight against her until she stopped struggling, Mrs. Nightingale took her daughter home.

She did nearly everything that she told her daughter she would do: she scrubbed Sally in the bathtub until there wasn't a trace of paint on her (instead, her skin was red from the intense scrubbing) and then she made Sally her favorite lunch: tuna fish with celery on a roll with Doritos and Pepsi. Neither mother nor daughter said a word to each other during the entire time and when Sally asked to be excused and went to her room, Mrs. Nightingale decided that she would not go out in search of Eddie. He would come home soon enough when he decided that he'd had enough of terrorizing the world and was hungry enough. It always happened. Why waste time searching throughout the winding surrounding neighborhood for a disobedient brat who could literally be hiding anywhere? He would be back, she surmised. She picked up her half-read paperback, sat down at the kitchen table and waited, not reading a word in front of her.

The phone rang twenty minutes later. It was Mr. Myers.

"I just wanted to let you know that I called the cops."

Mrs. Nightingale tried her best to sound nonchalant, as if she were fielding just another call from just another pissed-off victim of Eddie's mischief. "You didn't need to do that. I'm sorry about what Eddie did to your lawn and if there is anything I can do to fix it..."

He ignored her. "I knew they wouldn't believe me, but now they know that I tried to help. Now you know it too. You and they both know that I never wanted to hurt that boy or do anything to him. This wasn't my fault."

"Ben," she said, "when Eddie comes home, I'll have a full explanation from him as to what happened. Trust me."

"Just remember this when you decide to call the police," he said again. "Remind the police that I called them and that I had nothing to do with it." He hung up before she could say anything else to him.

Mrs. Nightingale called the police at exactly seven minutes to nine that night, just after she got back from looking all over the neighborhood for the son who hadn't come home.

* * *

Mr. Myers was brought in for questioning and his house was searched. The neighborhood came alive with the buzzing of voices confirming to each other that they always suspected that there was something wrong about Mr. Myers: too quiet, kept to himself too much, drank, don't you know. He's just the sort who would abscond with a child and do hateful things to it. Didn't he admit that he had shouted at the boy the morning he disappeared? And did you hear the story he's telling, that the boy just vanished into thin air right before his eyes? As if he expects anybody to believe that! No, they'll find that boy just as soon as they start digging up his cellar, you know, just like that awful John Wayne Gacy used to do. I always had my suspicions about him.

But nothing of Eddie, not his clothes, his bones nor the slingshot he always carried in his back pocket, ever turned up. Every search proved fruitless. And Mr. Myers *had* called the police even before the boy's mother had, even if the story was ridiculous. The boy's mother had confirmed everything that Mr. Myers told them, right down to the sharp smell in the air and the charred footprints in the grass, which nobody could make any sense of. And despite appearances, it was only paint that was splashed all over Mr. Myers' back lawn, not blood. Although there was no way Mr. Myers' version of events could have been the truth, there was no way he could be held in suspicion for the boy's disappearance.

And so the investigation continued. Everyone in the neighborhood was questioned about what they saw on that morning. Every story matched everyone else's and no one saw anything besides a paint-splattered little girl running down the street towards her mother. The more questions that were asked, the more the police got a full idea of what Eddie Nightingale was like: nobody in the neighborhood, from the oldest to the youngest, liked him. He was a troublemaker with a cruel laugh who seemed to thrive on other people's pain and embarrassment. It was possible that the boy annoyed the wrong person and something happened, either by plan or accident. It was too awful to even think about it, of course, him being so young and all, but the boy simply never listened to anyone. With knowing shakes of their heads, everyone commented that they could have predicted that the boy would come to something like this. And his poor mother, the poor suffering thing, to have her only son taken from her only two years after her husband passed away. What kind of world do we live in where things like this can happen?

After three months of investigation, the police were forced to conclude only one, horrible fact: on April 1st, 1976, ten year-old Eddie Nightingale disappeared off the face of the Earth without a trace.

* * *

On April 1st 2008, a car pulled up outside of a house on Garden Road and a forty year-old woman stepped out, looking sadly at the house that she hadn't gone near in over thirty years. In her childhood nightmares, she'd often seen the house outlined against the night sky, a hellish glow radiating all around it, its windows blank eyes and its front door an open maw that would open and gush something that she'd think at first was blood but always turned out to be red paint. She hated the color red: nothing she owned was red and she refused to live in any building that was painted red. When she'd gotten her first teaching position after college, she was horrified to discover that the school was painted red and she'd had to hold her breath and close her eyes every morning as she went in through the front door. That position had lasted only two months.

It had been a long time since Sally Nightingale had been in the old neighborhood; her mother, who'd practically broken her ribs with all the tight hugs she'd given her for the first year after Eddie disappeared, had finally decided to move only a few days after Mr. Myers put his grandfather's colt-45 against his right eye and made the last decision of his life. "Nightmares" said the note that was found beside him. And everyone in the neighborhood thought that had clinched it: obviously the guilt of what he had done to that boy had finally eaten him up. What else could he have had nightmares about, since there was no way that he was telling the truth about what he *said* he saw happen to that poor boy.

Even if there hadn't been a realtor's sign out front, letting her know that the house was empty, Sally still would have stopped the car and gotten out; she'd been thinking about coming here for months. Ever since her mother's death, she felt a need to come back and see it for herself just one time without her well-meaning mother telling her to look away and refusing to explain what she really thought happened to Eddie. The two of them had grown closer in the years following Eddie's disappearance, but Sally would've traded that wonderful bond in an instant just for the chance to sit down with her mother and have an actual, serious talk about what really happened that day. But it had been beyond the poor woman's power, and the unanswered questions had followed the both of them, nipping at the heels of happiness, ever since.

Sally took a deep breath, steeled herself, and walked around the side of the house until she found herself in the backyard, the early evening sun casting a warm and familiar radiance along the uncut grass that was thankfully no longer splattered with red paint. She nearly tripped in the tall grass as she made her way to the trees where she'd last seen Eddie with his mean smile and bulging paint balloon ready for launching. Bugs bit at her exposed shins, but she barely noticed:

all her focus was pointed at that spot she had barely caught a glimpse of all those years before when she was in her mother's arms.

Sally stepped forward and found she was not surprised to see that the grass was brown and dead in two spots, the footprints where Eddie had been standing when Mr. Myers saw him vanish.

Her chest hitched and the tears came to her eyes before she could stop them. Stupid, she thought, crying over something that happened so long ago. She clasped a hand against her mouth and cried harder, falling to her knees. She stayed in that position for a few minutes, with all the confusion and frustration spilling out of her and into the uncut grass.

"Mom," she said through the throb in her throat, "Eddie disappeared. Mr. Myers didn't kill him; nobody did! He disappeared! I don't know why, but he did!" She cried again, her heavy sobs coming out as moans that she didn't care if anybody heard. Nobody did.

After another few minutes, Sally felt herself drying up and she gathered the strength to get back to her feet. With a groan, she stood and turned away, going back the way she came. But after two steps, she stopped as she felt a bitingly cold breeze at her back.

What the…

And then it was in the air, in her nose; the smell that she'd gotten just the barest sniff of on that day, the same sharp, electrical smell. It tingled at the back of her nose and she sneezed. Her eyes grew wide as she turned back to the trees.

A tiny whirlwind of air formed just above the dead patches of grass and, with a quick flash of light like from an exploding flashbulb, her ten year-old brother, Eddie Nightingale, was standing in his thirty-two year-old footprints. He looked around himself, staring in wonder, before his eyes fell on the grown woman standing in front of him with her mouth hanging open in shock.

"Sally?" he asked.

Sally took a tentative step towards him and then stopped because she thought she might faint where she stood. "Eddie? Is it really you?"

No sooner were the words out of her mouth than Eddie's mouth widened into a horrible grin and he pointed at her, dancing around with glee. His laugh was as cruel as ever.

"Ha-Ha! I fooled you! April Fool, Sucker! Nyah-Nyah!"

EASTER

GOOD CAIAPHAS, THE COUNCIL WAITS FOR YOU

Judge Woodrow J. Hemingway, recently retired, had spent years addressing people while dressed in his black ceremonial robes and perched on a riser behind a tall desk. He'd passed sentence on many criminals while dressed in his robes and sitting at the head of his courtroom, feeling lofty but never showing it on his stern face. Consequently, there was never any occasion where he met with a defendant while dressed in nothing more impressive than his tan bathrobe or while perched on something as ordinary as the foot of his own bed. He never would have allowed a defendant, lawyer, bailiff, nor even his closest friends or his children to see him like this. He didn't even like it when his wife caught a glimpse of him before he had a chance to shave and dress. His morning look was his private look and no one was supposed to see him in that state. Which is why he was heartedly astonished to be staring at Corey Redding in exactly that state. Redding, called "Coriolanus" at his trial but referred to as Corey in the newspapers at the time of his arrest by journalists who didn't want to take the time to check the spelling of his full name, hadn't been there when the judge first woke up; the bedroom had been as it always was at eight o'clock in the morning: neat, pleasantly lit from the sunlight coming through the window, and above all, devoid of company. It was just the way he liked it. When his bladder finally told him that he could lie in bed no longer, he threw the covers aside, shuffled naked to his bathrobe lying on the floor, went into the bathroom to pee, and then only discovered Corey Redding sitting patiently in the chair opposite his bed when he came back out again. Judge Hemingway gasped and instinctively tightened the leather belt on his robe, which had been hanging open.

Redding's smile got bigger as his eyes stole a quick glance at what was dangling within the judge's robe before he closed it. He was dressed in an Angels' t-shirt and blue jeans, sitting back comfortably in the chair that the judge often used for quiet moments of contemplation by the window, which looked out onto his wife's garden one floor below. One leg was crossed over the other and he had his hands laced behind his head, looking relaxed. A stray thought flashed through the judge's head about how the last time Redding had probably had his hands behind his head was when he was arrested, although he couldn't have been as calm and relaxed then as he was now.

"What the Hell are you doing here?" the judge asked.

Redding shrugged. "Just dropped in to say 'Hi'. Damn, your Honor, what the Hell can you do with that little thing? No wonder you were in such a shitty mood throughout the trial."

The judge held his breath and felt his face go red. As the initial shock wore off, he could only shake his head as he searched for words.

"You can't possibly be here," he finally said.

Redding shrugged again, never dropping his smile. "Whatever you say, your Honor. Nice room you got here. Where do you keep the titty-mags?"

"No," the judge said, this time enunciating, "I said, you... can't... possibly... BE... HERE!"

"You can hear me, right?"

"That doesn't mean anyth…"

"And you can see me. What color are my eyes?"

The judge found himself answering against his better judgment. "Brown."

"There you go."

"But you *can't* possibly be here," the judge said again, hoping that somehow repeating that fact would make the intruder disappear. Redding only chuckled lightly.

"Fine," he said. "Then I'm impossibly here."

Judge Hemmingway's eyes stole a glance at the table on the other side of the bed, where the phone was. It was too far to reach and he wasn't a young man anymore, so leaping across the bed and getting a hold of it before Redding did was unlikely. Not impossible, but unlikely nevertheless.

"Need to make a call, your Honor?"

The judge forced himself to slip into his sternest expression, a product of years of training while sitting on the bench. "I suggest that you leave this room immediately. I don't know how you got in, but if you don't get out the same way, I'm gonna call the police."

"And tell them what?"

"That you escaped and broke into my home…"

Redding laughed. "Now come on, your Honor, you know as well as I do that I didn't escape and I sure don't see any evidence of breaking and entering, do you? The door ain't been forced, the windows ain't broken. No glass on the floor, no ladder leaning up against the house."

"You're sitting in my bedroom at 8:15 in the morning. That's evidence enough!"

Redding merely waved his hand, dismissing the logic. "You could have invited me over."

The judge scoffed despite his building rage. "Why the Hell would I invite you into my bedroom?"

"Maybe," Redding said, leaning forward, "you wanted to ask me what it felt like."

The judge's throat clicked and he started shaking his head, not wanting what was happening in front of him to be real, because if it was... that would mean...

"Darling," a voice belonging to Betty, the judge's wife, called from behind the door, "what do you want for breakfast?" The judge turned sharply at the sound of the voice and then back to Redding.

"Darling? She doesn't call you 'your Honor'?" Redding asked, giggling.

"Get out of here!"

"What was that?" Betty asked from behind the door.

"Nothing," the judge stammered, "I don't want anything. I'll make myself something later if I feel hungry."

There was a pause before she asked, "Are you alright, Woodrow?"

"I'm fine!"

"Oh, go on," said Redding, "ask her in."

"No!"

"What?" she asked.

"Nothing! Nothing at all! Don't come…"

But the door opened and the judge's sixty year-old wife came in, looking concerned. She gave the room a quick glance before turning her attention to her husband. "What's going on in here? You look as white as a sheet."

The judge stole a quick glance at Redding, sitting quietly across the room and smiling.

"Uh…"

"Are you trembling?"

The judge immediately straightened himself up and pretended that the tension had disappeared from his shoulders. "No Betty, I'm perfectly fine. I just…"

"What? What happened?"

"I… I feel so silly… another damn mouse just escaped under the bed. You know how much I hate those little pests!"

Redding giggled from his chair.

"Oh, not another one!" she said. "Where did you see it?"

The judge groaned at having to string the ridiculous lie out as long as he had to. "It scampered under the bed. It probably got past you and out the door."

Betty turned. "Oh no! I'll call the exterminator tomorrow."

"Thanks," he said a bit too loud because he wanted to be heard over Redding's laughter.

Betty was just about to leave when she said, "Now, are you sure that you don't want me to fix you anything?"

"I'm sure, dear. I just want to be by myself for a while."

Betty smiled. "I can't say I blame you; after an encounter with a mouse like that, I'd be pretty shaken up, too."

Redding roared with laughter.

"Dear…"

"I know," she giggled. "I was only kidding, you big baby. I'll see you when you come down. And don't take too long; the little ones will be over in a couple of hours to hunt for Easter Eggs. Try not to be Grouchy Gramps when they get here." She closed the door behind her and the two men were left alone. The judge finally turned his attention to Redding, who was shaking with uncontrollable laughter. The judge edged down to the foot of the bed, carefully sitting down and never taking his eyes off Redding. With little patience, he waited until Redding got a hold of himself.

"Oh, that was good, your Honor. If only everyone at the third district courthouse could've seen that! Eek, a mouse!" He seemed on the verge of collapsing into laughter again. The judge continued staring at him, a puzzle he couldn't solve and wasn't sure if he wanted to.

"She couldn't see or hear you."

Redding took a deep breath, wiped a tear away from his eye and finally stopped laughing. "That's right, Woody."

"Don't call me that."

Redding nodded. "You're absolutely right, your Honor. It ain't respectful, is it? So, 'your Honor', it is."

The judge looked away, trying to think. "You don't have to call me *that* either. I'm retired, now."

"Oh no, no. You're a man who's earned respect from ignorant black folks like me. I wouldn't think of showing you any disrespect, your Honor. Let it be said that Coriolanus Redding was nothing if not respectful."

The judge continued looking at the wall, not wanting to see the man in front of him, not wanting to accept what his presence in his bedroom meant. He chewed his tongue, an appalling habit he picked up in court whenever he suspected that a lawyer was trying to get around one of his rulings.

Redding leaned forward again. "So, do you want to know what it's like?"

"What?"

"Lethal injection; what the Hell else is there to talk about?"

The judge sat back a bit, not certain if he should continue down the path that Redding had started. Seeing no other way to continue, he said, "I would imagine that it doesn't feel like much of anything. Like going to sleep, they say."

For the first time, Redding's smile dropped.

"They're wrong."

"I was under the impression that they use a strong barbiturate to knock the patient out…"

"Patient? If that was an operation, it wasn't a successful one!"

"Don't interrupt me, Mr. Redding," the judge said, not liking to use Redding's name because it lent credibility to the very idea that he could be there in the bedroom. "I've never been an armchair general when it comes to sentencing. I've sat in many death houses watching a man that I've sentenced take his final seat, even back in the days when the chair had wires sticking out of it."

"Yeah, I know how many executions you've been to…"

"And I know for a fact," he said, talking over Redding, "that the first drug they administer, Sodium Thiopental, is meant to make the condemned lapse into unconsciousness, just like an operation."

Redding gave him a steady stare. "Yeah well, it *was* like an operation; like one of those operations that you hear about sometimes where the patient isn't completely out. You know what I'm talking about, don't you, your Honor? The type where a man is lying there, aware that they're cutting him to bits, feeling the knives slice him up, and he can't do nothin' to let them know he's awake. He just lies there, screaming inside." One of his eyes twitched, and the judge could see he was reliving his last moments right in front of him.

But he's not in front of me… I haven't woken up yet… In a few minutes, the grandkids will start stomping and shouting downstairs and wake me up and this time I won't mind at all… I'll scoop them up and kiss them all over their fat faces because otherwise it means that…

"I could hear everything around me, too," Redding continued. "And just before my heart seized up, I heard you make a noise."

"I didn't say a word during…"

"It was a grunt… and it sounded very satisfied. You know, like 'Good riddance to bad garbage'."

The judge stood up and started for the head of the bed. "Look, I don't have much time…"

"Grandkids and Easter Eggs," said Redding and then chuckled. "So it's Easter today? I guess that makes sense: kill a man on Good Friday and there's no reason to be surprised when Easter comes along and you find in your bedroom…"

But the judge cut him off as he climbed back under the covers, forgetting to take off his robe. "No, you don't understand; I'm going to be waking up soon."

"Come on, your Honor; do you really think you're just dreaming me up? You think I'm the pastrami on rye that you had last night?"

That proves it, the judge thought; only a dream would know what I had to eat last night. "As you can see, Mr. Redding; I'm getting into bed and closing my eyes. In a moment, you'll disappear into a fog and I'll wake up and you'll be just as dead as you were yesterday. So if you've turned up in my dreams to tell me something, you'd better say it fast." So saying, he laid back, pulled the covers up to his chin and closed his eyes.

The room was silent for a moment and the judge thought that his plan had worked, that his nighttime phantom had gone to the same place as the boogeyman had gone when he was eight years-old. The judge snuggled into his pillows and his formally pinched face relaxed.

Then the voice was right against right ear. "I'm not going anywhere, your Honor."

He's not there… stop shaking because it's all just a dream…

"You see, when a man is dying of a heart attack and can't even scream because of the drugs, he does a lot of thinking; it's the only thing he can do. And when I heard you grunt, I started thinking about you."

The judge started slowly pulling the covers up over his head. "You're blaming me for your sentence? The jury found you guilty and that lawyer of yours wasn't the best that ever stood before me."

"I was thinking about him too, about how he turned green when he found out you were gonna be presiding over my case. I had to bug him for a half hour before he told me you had a reputation… 'kind of a hanging judge,' he said."

The judge's voice started to tremble. "Don't be ridiculous."

"And he pointed out that this was going be your last case. He didn't come right out and say that you might want one last go at sending a man to the needle, no matter what the circumstances."

The covers were now up to his nose. "Are you telling me that you didn't stab that twenty year-old kid?"

"Oh, I did it alright, in self-defense!"

"The jury didn't buy that."

"You wouldn't let them."

"Don't be ridic…" But suddenly, the judge felt the covers resist his efforts to cover his head completely. He struggled, but they were being pulled down.

He's grabbed them! Oh my God, he's really here!

"Judge, I went to the death chamber and didn't come out again. The last thing I am is ridiculous. If anything, I know more now than I ever have in my whole life. Now open your Goddamn eyes and tell me how ridiculous I am!"

The judge squeezed his eyes tighter.

"Open them or I'll rip them out!"

"You're not really…"

"You don't really believe that, do you? Now let's see those baby blues."

The judge opened his eyes and the face of the man who had never been closer to him than the distance from the bench to the defendant's table was close enough for the judge to feel his breath, that is, if any breath could come out of a dead man's face. The lack of breath against his nose confirmed the worst for the judge; he was face to face with a corpse, some corporeal ghost who'd crawled out of the depths of Hell to present his case to him.

I thought I'd sat on my last case already, but here it is right now! God, help me…

Redding's face was twisted and crimped in pure hatred. The judge realized that he could do nothing but hear the man out.

"Self-defense?" the judge asked in a whisper.

"He was mugging me at knifepoint."

"But he was the one who got stabbed." The judge kept his tone even, not wanting to provoke Redding any further.

"I fought back; I'm good at fighting."

"I know; you had a record of street gang fights and muggings a mile long."

"It's been four years since I've been in trouble."

The judge had heard arguments like this before and let his nature get the better of him. "You mean it's been four years since you've been *caught*."

Redding whipped the covers off him in one swipe, leaving the judge flat on his back and cringing in his bathrobe and belt. "I know that's what you thought. That's why you wouldn't let my lawyer do his job. Every time he tried to argue my case, all you said was 'immaterial' and 'irrelevant'. And then there was 'Get to the point, Mr. Tucker'. You must have said that twenty times! And then when you summed up for the jury, I could hear what you were really telling them: 'You can't really believe him, you know'. 'They're born liars and killers, all of them!'"

The judge tried to push himself further into the mattress with no success. "That boy you murdered... he'd never been in trouble before..."

"You mean he was never *caught* before."

"There was no reason to believe your story. He was young, was going to college..."

"He was white." For this, the judge had no answer. The two men, the dead man and the man who was sure he was dead, stared at each other. The judge scrunched closer to the headboard and realized that if this was his last moment of life, he would refute the charges against him to the end, just as so many men in the death room did just before the buttons were pushed.

"I can't expect you to agree, Mr. Redding. I did my job the best that I could do and the opinion of one man, even a man whom I sent to death row, isn't going to change my mind about that."

Redding stood over him, his face twitching. Then he smiled and the judge knew he was a dead man. "But this isn't just one man's opinion, your Honor. There are a few others…"

The judge's mouth dropped open. "What are you talking about?"

"Get up."

"No!"

"GET UP!" Redding grabbed the judge's robe and pulled him out of bed with hardly a grunt. Before the judge realized it, he was standing on his feet in front of the corpse.

This is it!

But it wasn't it. Instead, Redding pulled the judge over to the window, whipping him with enough strength to rebound the judge off the wall. The judge grabbed the hand that he'd used to brace himself in pain.

"Ahhgh!" he yelled. "I think you broke my finger!"

Redding ignored this. "Look outside."

The judge looked and his breath stopped at the sight of the crowd of people standing on the back lawn, looking resolutely up at him with glazed eyes and dried, dead skin. Although he could not call many of their names to mind, he recognized each and every one of the multitude of faces. Some of the faces were black, some Hispanic, and even a few that would have fallen into his father's definition of "white trash". Worst of all, he could see quite clearly that the ones in the back sported burnt skin from their trip in the electric chair. In front of them, the corpses were blue from the strangulating gases that he'd sentenced them to breath. In front were the injection victims, largely unchanged from their living selves except the slack-jaws and the zombie-like way they stood and rocked back and forth, as if a good strong breeze would knock them all over. It was a panorama of the condemned as the penalty became more humane over all the years.

He barely noticed his throbbing finger as he uncontrollably gripped the window frame tighter; his mind was too full of the faces in front of him and his ears equally as full of the voice behind him.

"In a way," said Redding, "I'm lucky. After all, I got that trial that I had no hope of walking away from; in some countries you don't even get that. And then there was the way they executed me: I mean, dying of a drug-induced heart attack while fully aware is a real bitch, to be honest, but it could have been a lot worse. In the old days, I would have been electrocuted, or beheaded, or crucified like Jesus... of course, he came back on Easter. Funny how things work out sometimes, ain't it?"

The judge couldn't say anything; so engrossed was he in the crowd of the condemned who had refused to stay dead that he never noticed Redding's hands reach around and undo his belt buckle.

"I could have even been hanged."

Redding slipped the belt from around the judge's waist.

Fight back, you idiot! Tell him... tell all of them... they're wrong! They're the ones' who broke the law... they're the murderers, not you! You represent the law and justice and... this just can't be the way it ends!

But the judge never moved, even when he saw the belt briefly pass in front of his eyes.

* * *

Betty Hemingway ate a light breakfast, considered knocking on her husband's door one more time to see if he felt like coming down, and decided to let him do his own thing in his own time, just like he always did throughout their marriage. She reflected that sometimes it was no fun being married to a judge: they got their way all the time at work and tended to demand the same when they got home. Still, after all these years, she'd gotten used to it and hoped that now that Woodrow was retired, he might lose a few of his old bad habits and finally become the type of manageable husband that she dearly needed now that she was in her Autumn years. And until that day came, she still had her hobbies to keep her busy and out of the way of Woodrow's incessant demands, like working in the garden. And didn't that sound like just the way to spend this lovely Easter morning, especially since Janis and the grandkids wouldn't be over for another hour. She smiled to herself, laced dirty sneakers onto her feet, and put on a wide straw hat to protect her from the sun before stepping into the backyard.

The yard looked lovely and she breathed in the fresh clean air, feeling alive and good. It was only when she turned around to inspect the azaleas that she saw her husband hanging like Judas by his neck from his belt, the other end jammed into the closed second floor window. Betty dropped her trowel as her horrified mind realized that his bathrobe was fluttering open in the breeze and his mid-sixties naked body could clearly be seen by anyone who cared to look. Quite clearly from the ground, she could see that a note with one word – GUILTY – was pinned to the robe of the hanging judge.

MOTHER'S DAY

HUSH, LITTLE BABY

Stan Fisher was just picking up his double latte from the service counter when he looked to his right and saw the woman's worried face. He thought it such a strange sight since everyone else in the coffee shop was either reading, tapping away on their laptops or holding animated conversations with their friends. Since hers was the only face amongst the many to just be staring off into space and looking as if the world was going to crash down on her once-pretty little head, his attention was captured. And yes, Stan could tell that her face was definitely once a pretty one. She didn't really look any older than him, but trying times had carved their memoirs into her skin. Plus, her hair, which had a few strands of gray in it, was tied back and she was dressed in sweat clothes and flip-flops. There wasn't a hint of any color that wasn't her natural color on her face, in her hair or on her fingers and toes. Only by taking a moment to imagine what she must have looked like before the hard times hit her did he realize that he knew who she was.

Stan took a few steps towards her, not sure if he should interrupt her reverie. She might be embarrassed to be seen by someone who knew her as she was, he thought. But his certainty that what this woman needed now was a friend won out.

He cleared his throat. She didn't notice. Haltingly, he said, "Cindy?"

She still didn't notice and, for a moment, he thought he may have been wrong. He tried again. "Cindy?"

The woman suddenly looked up into his eyes with such a piercing, searching stare that Stan felt like mumbling an apology and running away, no matter if it was Cindy or not. Then her sadness cleared.

"I know you, don't I?" she asked.

"Stan Fisher," he said. "We both went to UCLA, same graduating class. Remember? I used to play guitar outside the library and you and your friends would sing."

Her memory jogged, she stood up and looked him up and down, shocked that this pleasant memory had suddenly visited her out of nowhere. "Stan Fisher, yes I remember you." She grabbed his forearms as if testing to see if he was really there in front of her.

"Cindy 'Songbird' Grant. How are you?"

She giggled. "Nobody's called me that since college."

"Well, it was true then. You had the best voice of the whole bunch. And you actually knew all the lyrics to all those obscure folk songs that I liked to play."

She simply smiled and looked at him, happy to see him but apparently at a loss for anything to say. He broke the moment by saying, "Would you mind if I joined you for a bit?"

"Oh, please," she said, genuinely excited. He sat down in the empty chair opposite hers and took a sip from his latte. She did the same and he saw her face make a tiny grimace.

"Is your coffee cold?" he asked. "You want another one?"

"No, I… to tell you the truth I don't like coffee much, but you have to buy something so that they'll let you sit here and I just had to get out of the apartment. So, how are you doing? What are you up to?"

"Oh fine," he said, sitting back with his cup. "I work freelance writing jingles for commercials. It pays the bills so that I can get into the studio from time to time and put another of my boring songs on tape. And you?"

She sighed tiredly in answering. "I work from home as a telemarketer. Not the most interesting job in the world. Still, it's good to hear that you're still making music. You haven't changed a bit."

Stan was bringing the cup to his lips again but paused, realizing that he was stuck for something to say. He opened his mouth and closed it again.

"It's alright," she said. "You don't have to say it back. I know what I look like."

Stan changed the subject. "So what have you been up to? Husband, kids… Did some little one make you a Mother's Day card today?"

Cindy's face immediately clouded over, as if she'd just been reminded about how her favorite grandmother died a lingering death from stomach cancer. She looked exactly the same as she did when he first spotted her and he realized that he must have accidently struck at the sorest spot of her problems. "I'm sorry; I didn't mean to pry…"

Cindy was quick to stop him. "No, no, you had no idea. In fact, I've been looking for someone to…" She faltered, glanced out the window and then said, "Do you have some time?"

At first, Stan considered lying and looking at his watch for maximum effect in order to get out of hearing whatever this poor, tired, beaten woman had to tell him. But the memory of Cindy as she had once been, bright eyed and vivacious as she sat next to him on the campus and sang "Pack Up Your Sorrows" in a voice that would have shamed Joan Baez into silence, kept him seated. He had to find out what kind of road a person had to walk to turn her into an old woman by the age of thirty-seven. Taking a deep breath, he said, "Does this have to do with your mother? Is she ill?"

"No," she said, staring out the window again, "it has nothing to do with my mother."

"You have a child, then."

"Yes. I'm raising it on my own."

"You're divorced?"

"No."

"I see. It was an accident."

She fixed her stare at him. "The only accident I made was walking through the park alone. I was raped."

All at once, the image that he'd had of Cindy "Songbird" Grant as her pretty voice harmonized with his on a hundred old songs cracked and shattered before his eyes. Something ugly turned over in his mind and he imagined himself kicking a faceless deviant into the pavement until he gave one last groan and stopped moving.

"Who did it?"

Cindy's eyes watered up, but no tears fell. "They never found out. I never saw his face."

Stan sat back and blew out a long breath. "So, you decided to have it."

"My mother decided for me. She told me I would go to Hell if I committed 'the greatest sin', as she called it. She also let it be known that I would no longer be welcome in her home. I couldn't bear to lose my mother, so…"

"That took a lot of guts. Is the baby with your mother now?"

Cindy leaned forward and started to rock gently, her gaze fixed on an invisible point in space. "I haven't seen or talked to my mother in three years, ever since the baby was born."

Stan couldn't believe what he'd just heard; it was like being told that dogs had been the dominant species on Earth all along. "You mean she abandoned you even after you did what she asked you to do? How could she possibly…"

"I don't blame her." Cindy fixed her stare on him again and he tried as hard as he could to read her face. What kind of upbringing had she had to produce a grown woman who believed she deserved to be so violently abused? Stan decided he would try to clear the air with a simpler question.

"What's his name, or is it a her?"

"It doesn't have a name."

"Three years old and you still haven't come up with a name?"

"There's no way I could name it. There's no way I could describe…"

"You keep saying 'It'."

Cindy looked at the table, breathed deeply and said, "My child… isn't normal. It does things… horrible things." After a moment, she peeked up at him to see his reaction. "You think I'm crazy, don't you? I can see it in your eyes."

He gritted his teeth before answering. "Cindy, have you ever talked to anyone else about this, like maybe a therapist or someth…"

"Maybe you'd better go," she said, turning to the window.

"I just think it might help you if you just…"

"Please, go."

She refused to look at him, although he could tell that there was no sternness or hatred in her dismissal of him, only disappointment. He started to rise, but never stood up fully.

Look at her. She just needs you to listen. Remember how your heart used to beat whenever you saw her coming your way.

He sat back down again. "No, I'm not gonna go. I'm gonna sit here and shut up and let you tell me what you have to tell me. I'll bite my lip whenever I get the urge to interrupt you. I'm ready."

Cindy turned back to him and this time there was a tear rolling down her face. "I'm still not sure, Stan."

"I told you I wouldn't…"

"No, it's just that… it could be dangerous for you…"

Something on the back of Stan's neck tingled, but he had sat down and knew he wouldn't get up again until he knew everything.

"Tell me," he said.

So she did.

* * *

"It was Mother's Day when I felt the first contraction and went to the hospital. The labor lasted hours. When the baby was born, I fainted a second after I heard the nurse scream and hit the floor. Just before I passed out, I felt a glancing pain down between my legs and there was a scratching there like dull stones scrabbling at me. I've always had trouble remembering my dreams whenever I wake up in the morning, but while I was out I had this terrible vision of a rabid puppy leaping up on top of me and going for my throat. It's never left me. I felt like I was screaming and nobody would come to help me, not my mother, not the doctors, not anyone; I was all alone with this thing tearing my neck open and slobbering foam all over me. When I woke up, I instinctively reached for my throat. But I've had that dream many times since then and I'll never get used to it. Not a week goes by that I don't wake up in the middle of the night gasping and scared.

I looked around my room and saw a nurse sitting in the furthest corner from me, staring at me as if I was something profane. I remember feeling confused and angry at her, but later when I found out what happened, I couldn't blame her. I asked her where my baby was and if I could talk to the doctor. She got up and edged past the bed, never taking her eyes off me, before she got to the door and ran down the hall. I think that was the first time I was really scared. It's awful when you wake up in a hospital bed, dizzy and exhausted, and all you see is this frightened woman in front of you. I closed my eyes and prayed that everything was alright. It was the last time I ever prayed.

The doctor came in a few minutes later, wheeling in what looked like a box covered with a towel on a gurney. At that moment, I was sure that my baby was dead and that its little body was underneath the towel. I'd be lying if I said that I was sorry to think that that was what happened; I never wanted that baby, as I already told you, and it dying naturally would've been the only way to satisfy my mother. That's what I was waiting for the doctor to say, but then I noticed his hands: they were both heavily bandaged. He was wincing when he pushed the gurney to the foot of the bed.

'Doctor, what happened to you?' I asked, but he wouldn't tell me. I then asked him if my mother was in the hospital chapel. I figured she would've found out about its death and would be praying. The doctor simply shook his head and said, 'She left. She didn't say where she was going, but she didn't look like she had any intention of coming back.' I couldn't believe what I was hearing. I was about to ask the doctor what he was talking about, but that's when we both heard the sound underneath the towel.

It was a low, drawn-out snarl and the box jiggled on the gurney, like whatever was underneath the towel was rolling around and hitting the sides of the box. The doctor turned white and he said, 'We sedated it, but it's wearing off.'

I felt like everything I had ever eaten in my life was coming up my throat. All I could say was, 'My baby…' The doctor just mumbled that he was sorry and left the room in a hurry.

The box jiggled more and that snarl was coming out of it like regular breaths. I was still dizzy, but I got on my knees and crawled to the end of the bed, where the box was sitting within reach. It wouldn't stop making that noise and it took everything I had to get myself to lift that towel off the box and look in.

They'd tied it up with someone's belt, so its arms were pressed against its sides. Its eyes were wide open and the red pupils looked up at me with dumb hatred. My hand was frozen in the air, the grip solid on the towel, no matter how much I wanted to cover it up again. I looked away from its eyes and saw its tiny fingers twiddling and the light reflected off the tiny, rounded claws that were sticking out of its fingertips. Although its skin was mostly smooth and pink, I could see the very beginning of small teardrops forming all over its body that I knew would someday harden into scales. There was nowhere I could look and see a normal baby. Those were the claws that had scrabbled at me on the operating table. And the pain I'd felt…

And I remembered the doctor's bandaged hands. I looked down between my legs and saw light bite marks in an oval on the inside of my thigh.

That's when the constant snarl became a growl. It opened its mouth and I saw the crooked row of tiny, pointed teeth."

* * *

Cindy paused and took another sip of her tepid coffee, just to wet her mouth. Stan sat still opposite her, biting his lip.

* * *

"The staff let me know in no uncertain terms that I was free to leave as soon as I felt able to stand and walk. When that wasn't quick enough for them, they wheeled me and the box into an ambulance and ran at least twelve red lights to get me home. When the ambulance peeled out of there, leaving me with the covered box moaning and thrashing in my arms, I knew that no one was going to help me.

I hurried into my apartment before anyone could take a good look at me and found a note lying on the kitchen table. It was from my mother: I won't go into all the Bible verses she mixed-up and misquoted, but the point of the note was to tell me that she always knew I would come to this, sinful creature that I was and that I now had my own little monster to care for and see if I would like it anymore than she did. So I just sat there at the table, the box shaking around. And then the growling became more high-pitched and I realized that it was demanding to be fed. There was no way I was going to stick my breast anywhere near those teeth, so I got up and prepared a bottle as quickly as I could, the thing's cries growing louder and the box rocking back and forth so violently that I thought it might tip over and spill him loose, and that was the last thing that I wanted. When the bottle was ready, I leaned over the box and it seemed to calm slightly but there was still a look in those red eyes, as if it knew that it needed me but that its patience was only going to last a little longer. I lowered the bottle into the box and it lunged up and caught the nipple in its jaws, tearing it off and drenching itself in formula. It screamed, not the way babies' scream when they want something, but like a wild animal frustrated that it can't climb a tree to get at the prey that it chased up there in the first place. Its little arms struggled with the belt and I could hear the leather creak as it tore slightly. The thought of the little beast free and tearing around the kitchen scared me so much that I just ran to the refrigerator to see if there was anything in there that would placate it. Sitting right in front of me was a plastic container of leftover hamburger and macaroni that my mother made three nights before. If I had been thinking clearly, I would never have allowed myself to consider that stuff as baby food. Only a maniac would ever have considered putting that cold, leftover muck in a baby's mouth. But the baby howled louder and I heard the belt giving way just a little bit more and all sensible thought was gone. I grabbed the container and a spoon from the sink and rushed back to the box. The belt was nearly torn and its jaws were thrashing so much that it was drawing blood from its own lips. In another moment it would break free and, like the rabid dog in my dream, it would be on top of me. I spooned up a bit of the casserole and held it to the baby's snapping jaws.

It stretched its head up and took the food, biting the head of the spoon clean off! I just sat there, my mouth stupidly hanging open, hoping it would choke on the spoon and I could be free of it. It chewed, worked the food and the spoon around in its mouth for a minute, and then spat the crumpled metal up and out of the box. Its teeth made mincemeat of the thing. A moment later, it swallowed all it was chewing and then looked up at me, its mouth open and waiting for more. I just held the plastic container over its head and gently spilled the rest of the mixture into its mouth. It snapped and chewed, snapped and chewed, gulped and swallowed like a garbage disposal and only slowed down when the container was nearly empty. Then its head fell back and it gurgled, completely sated. I had to wait for my heart to stop beating hard before I could look at it again; its stomach had swelled, but instead of crying in pain like a normal baby would, it just laid on its back and let out a huge belch.

Thirty minutes later, it all came out the other end. I won't say anymore about that.

Forty minutes after that, it was hungry again."

* * *

Someone sat down at the table next to Cindy and Stan with an extra-large mocha and opened a newspaper. Without a word, the two of them sat back up in their chairs, reached over for whatever discarded magazines that were lying around, and pretended to read them.

Exactly twenty-four minutes went by before the interloper finished his coffee and left. Almost simultaneously, Cindy and Stan put down their magazines and leaned towards each other again.

* * *

"Over the last three years, I saw it change and grow and learned what I could do to keep it contented enough not to hurt anyone. And when I say change, I mean things like those teardrop patterns on its skin, which hardened into scales just like I'd predicted on the day it was born. The only place scales didn't form was its head and a long stripe down its spine; that's where the hair came in within the first four months. And it *has* grown: in three years it's grown like you could never imagine.

To this day, it can't talk; I don't think that its vocal chords have developed to any degree and I don't think they ever will. It understands the things that I say to it; I'm certain of it. It just chooses to ignore me. And when it does dismiss me, it does so with this terrible laugh that sounds like a cobra hissing. The first time I heard it, I nearly jumped out of my shoes.

The darkness seems to calm it, maybe because of its first memory of being covered in that dark box by the doctor. When I tried to hang black drapes in the window, it made a sound I hope I never hear again. It knew what I was trying to do and, although it'll allow me some degree of peace during the course of the day, it didn't like the idea that I was trying to keep it quiet. Besides, dark or light, it knows when it gets hungry and it tells me when it wants to be fed.

As for food, it quickly tired of the meat that I was preparing for it four times during the day and once at eleven o'clock at night. It'll settle for it for a while, but eventually it wants something special. It found a way to communicate with me. Back when I thought I was going to have a human child, someone made me a gift of flash cards that had pictures of animals, people and objects with the name of it underneath: a teaching tool. Every once in a while it'll slip a card underneath the door. The card will say something like "bird" or "cat" and I know that it will not be satisfied until I get it exactly what it asked for. Worst of all, I found out that when it wants something special, it wants it alive. I can't tell you how many times my heart's broken because I carried a cute cat or a guinea pig down that hallway, opened the door and tossed it in. And then I run back with my hands over my ears, not wanting to hear the poor little thing scream when that creature catches it.

I don't know why I haven't killed it yet; I've wanted to a million times over the years. I want to buy a gun and shoot it as many times as I can, then reload and shoot it some more. I've thought about soaking its food in Draino or just setting fire to the whole building and screw anyone who happens to be home at the time. But something's happened: maybe it's my imagination, but I sometimes think it can hear my thoughts and the growls and the grunts are its answers and I know what it's saying. I can hear words in that low, guttural noise. It says, 'Try anything and I'll get you first. You can run away, but I'll always be faster than you, Mommy. Because I'm your sin and all the blood in every man, woman and child can't wash it away. When I finally decide to send you to Hell, you'll be grateful to burn. I promise you, I will send you there but in my own good time.'"

* * *

Cindy sat back in her chair, spent and saddened at reliving the whole experience again. She stared at Stan, trying to discern what was going on behind that horrified, incredulous expression.

"You don't believe me, do you?" she asked.

He just sat in front of her, apparently turning the entire story around in his head. It was only after a few moments that he seemed to shake himself out of his trance.

"I... I don't know what to think."

"Do you think that I would make up something like that to someone I haven't seen in fifteen years? Does that make sense to you?"

Stan slowly stood up, not looking at her. "I'm sorry, Cindy; I've got to go."

As he turned away, her voice became more worried. "But I can prove it, every word! I live just two blocks away! You can see it for yourself..."

Stan quickly turned back and his shocked eyes told her that he had no intention of letting her prove her story to him. He shook his head and looked down, averting her stare.

"I should have told you how I felt about you in college," he said. "I was too shy. You were gorgeous then. And you could sing like nobody's business."

"Stan, if you have any feelings for me at all, you'll let me prove it to you. I'm not crazy! I need someone to believe me! Just come home with me and..."

Stan's hand was up in front of her face and it stopped her. "I should have told you then. Maybe we could've been together and you wouldn't be in this spot. You can blame me, if you like... whatever. But it's too late. I'm sorry for what happened to you, but I'm going now."

"But..."

"You won't see me here anymore," he said as he headed for the door. He didn't look back or look in the window as he passed her for the last time on his way down the street. He hated himself for leaving her, knew that she wanted just one person in the world to believe her, to help her cope, but it was beyond him. Maybe she was crazy; maybe the horrors of her attacker and her mother gave birth to a fantasy so strong that all he would find if he went to her apartment would be the rotted corpse of a starved, badly-neglected but otherwise perfectly normal baby.

But something told him that was not what he would find there.

Stan got home ten minutes later, picked up his guitar and started playing as loud as he could. In an hour, he'd written a song: "Death of a Songbird."

* * *

When Stan walked out of the coffee shop, Cindy choked back a sob and turned her face away to the window so that none of the customers would notice her. She cursed herself for what she had tried to do and was relieved that Stan had not taken her up on her invitation. She remembered the happy times they'd had, sitting on the grass with a few friends and singing, a simple and pure expression of the joy that they thought would last forever. She'd noticed the times he'd looked at her longer and more warmly than usual and often thought about taking the first step. But neither of them had and, as he said, it was too late.

He'd made the right decision and she was glad that she wouldn't have to find out what it felt like to lead Stan down the hallway.

She placed a hand to her stomach; the cold coffee was cramping it. It was almost as bad as it had been that morning when she found the flashcard lying just in front of the creature's bedroom door. She didn't bother to look at the drawing because it was the three-letter word that captured all her attention: MAN.

Knowing that there wasn't much time left before it would lose its patience, Cindy decided to do what she had originally planned; her trip to the coffee shop had been just a necessary means of coming to grips with what she was about to do. She reached into her pocketbook, pulled out her cell phone and dialed. She spoke as evenly as her trembling nerves would allow when the call was answered.

"Mr. Grimaldi? This is Cindy Grant in 206. I'm fine, but I have a problem: a baseball came through the bedroom window this morning. I know you won't have a replacement available, but do you think you could take the shattered pane away? No, I cleaned up the glass from the floor, but I didn't want to touch the pane. It looked kind of dangerous. You can? When? Twenty to thirty minutes at the most? I'm not calling from the apartment; I had to go on a few errands and I'll be a while. You can let yourself in, can't you? Great, I appreciate it. I'll be back in a couple of hours. Thank you so much. Bye-bye."

Problem solved, she thought as she hung up. Although she didn't know what she would do the next time the MAN card came under the door, she would find a way to get it what it wanted, especially since she knew that there was a card in that deck that read MOMMY.

Someday, that card would be lying there and the door would open and...

Cindy got herself another coffee and sat in the coffee shop for another thirty minutes. At the thirty-first minute, she left the shop and started walking home.

MEMORIAL DAY

THE MERRY WIDOW WALTZ

Only a few people lived in the general area of Stoneridge Cemetery, and those that did went through the usual trouble of trying to sell their houses. The many empty houses that had not fallen into decay on Parker Street had been abandoned by the wealthier inhabitants who had decided that they could afford a second house before selling the first. One recently deserted house that had begun to fall into disarray, 12 Parker Street, was not yet on any of the realtor's books. Edith Babcock had neglected to contact anyone to explain that she was leaving. No one on Parker Street had even realized that she was gone until Warren Bennett, the delivery man for Newberry Dairy Products, saw his deliveries from the day before spoiling on her doorstep.

Warren Bennett was far from pleased with his discovery; he usually tried to complete the Parker Street leg of his route in the shortest possible time and some days had to restrain himself from just tossing the bottles of milk at the front porches while speeding by them. Today, a bottle of neglected milk on a doorstep told him that he would be forced to spend more time than he wanted on Parker Street.

Mrs. Babcock was indeed gone, and her body sprawled in her foyer at the foot of a tall staircase confirmed it. After three days, the acrid stench of death was powerful yet nowhere near as heavy and oppressive as the cloud of death that surrounded Stoneridge Cemetery and most of the houses located on Parker Street. It was the sticky, suffocating air that every resident of Parker Street drew in with each morning yawn. Warren Bennett could feel it weighing down in his lungs every morning when he hurried through his route. The stagnant, dead air that hung over the houses and drove the tenants away was a cloud of decay that Edith Babcock had ceased enduring and had begun to add to as she moved across the street into Stoneridge Cemetery.

It would only be natural to assume that the saddened visitors to Stoneridge were forced to deal with the choking atmosphere, that is if one didn't know that the small plot of dismal land found itself continually short of mourners. Since Herbert McManus, the ground-breaker of Stoneridge, was first lowered into his resting place twenty-three years earlier, the cemetery had become a home for the friendless and the lonely; a garbage dump of bones that was reserved for only those whose last selfish thoughts confirmed that no tears would fall at their burial. Stoneridge remained a sanctuary for the lonesome dead, and only those who had ostracized human kindness from their lives were allowed into the cool, tender clutches of the roots that snaked through the earth and its children.

On the evening of May 25th, Memorial Day, the sullen gloom of the cemetery broke momentarily - as it did every Memorial Day - by the sound of a motor dying just in front of its iron gates. The crooked, overhanging branches waved excitedly at the presence of a living person, one that chugged up every year in her virgin-white Volkswagen to perform her yearly chore as a dutiful widow.

Carol Crantz - at one time Carol Simon (before the mistake occurred, she would say) - felt the nerves running down her back tickle uneasily as she hit the emergency brake. Her headlights clicked off, and only the dim dusk allowed her to discern the craggy fingers of the dying, leafless trees and the shadowed humps that were the tombstones. Carol needed neither the sunlight nor her headlights to find the stone she was looking for.

She opened the car door and the swollen smog of death

surrounded her. It rushed up into her nostrils before her unprepared body could adjust. The musk swirled inside her head, sending her into a brief swoon. She shook herself awake and took shorter breaths, only forcing herself out of the comfort and normality of her car when she felt blood flowing through her head again. Her feet sank into the soft earth and dead leaves that littered the area. Carol guessed with certainty that the city had given up on the stretch of land in which so many forgotten bones lay; the litter of decomposed leaves and twigs would never remain in a cemetery that contained even one missed loved one.

"Six stones up, two to the left," she chanted under her breath as she walked through the uninviting gates. The mud clutched at her shoes, nearly pulling the right one off; it pulled greedily at her like a miser reaching for one last silver dollar. Almost stumbling as she pulled herself loose from the mud, she continued on, never looking directly at the stones she passed and holding a white handkerchief to her nose to filter the smell. Mechanically, she felt her way past the sinking, cracked stones until the legend, carved in the stone, stood steadfast in front of her:

STEWART L. CRANTZ

b. 1967 - d. 2003

There were no R.I.P. initials carved into the stone: she had not allowed it. And they refused to permit the initials that she felt more appropriate: B.I.H. - Burn In Hell. Henceforth, neither a hopeful nor damning epitaph was given to Stewart L. Crantz: he resided in perpetual doubt.

Five years would've seemed like a long time (to most of her friends who, fortunately, knew nothing of this yearly practice) to burn in the rage of her marriage, and this year was not the first to have thoughts of "giving it a rest" creep into her mind. But the mirrors that hung all over her house fueled her fiery anger; she was not a young woman any longer: her deep black hair sported streaks of light gray and the lines dug by the thousands of tears lay deeply embedded in her face. Marriage was a life sentence.

She had heard most of her friends scream the words to their husbands during periods of impossible frustration: the Sunday afternoon football games, the torn trousers, the late nights after work, et cetera. The eyes staring up to heaven and the sudden burst of shaking, as if trying to suppress what demanded to be let out, usually preceded the oath:

"Just wait: when you're dead, I'll dance on your grave!"

The air, pouring into her lungs like pea-soup reminds her that she does not want to spend any more time at this desolate grave than necessary. It has already gotten much darker than she is comfortable with. Her breath holds as she slips off her shoes and places her bare feet into the wet grass sprouting from her husband's grave. The dew chills the soles of her feet and sends electricity up her back. Her rationale is sleeping as, with eyes closed tight, she skips and bounces shyly on the plot of earth that covers her husband's body.

Her words barely hiss from between her teeth as she flutters slowly upon the grave. "I'll dance on your grave, I swear!"

Like last year and the year before, Carol suddenly tires. Her arms hang limply and jounce with her every step and her bones shiver like they will collapse inside her body. But while her legs cry out for rest, she will not sit down because she knows that she will sink into the grave, slowly and with her guard lowered, and he will be there with his raised eyebrows and his haunted eyes. She dances faster.

"I'll dance on your grave, see? I'm doing it! I'll be happy without you and I'll dance..."

Carol put her left foot down hard and a twinge forced her to stop short. She knew she was bleeding as she sat back heavily against the stone, holding her foot as she tried to inspect it in the darkness. A thin line of blood trickled from the cut. Carol sat back, trying to force her eyes to pick through the darkened grass to find what she had stepped on.

She could not find any tiny shards of glass or metal. Her confusion lasted only a second and was swallowed by a cloud of exhaustion floating in front of her eyes, slowly teasing them shut. She vaguely wondered if he had somehow reached up through the ground and she stepped on his reaching fingernail, a thought that should have sent her screaming back to the car, but the exhaustion nailed her to the stone. The strength that she had built into her heart drained smoothly from her and left behind the same woman who had buried her husband five years earlier: a woman who'd lost a man who had never slunk past his own house on the way to the local bar, who had never stormed in at three in the morning with a loud laugh and uncertain legs, who had never sat hypnotized in front of a television for an entire day and tipped can after can of Pabst Blue Ribbon down his throat.

He'd never had the time; the marriage had lasted only three months.

Carol Crantz was again the woman who wanted to know why.

"You're here, aren't you?"

(yes)

Carol bent over and hid her face in her hands. The tears of the newlywed Carol Crantz returned with vigor as if she had never forgotten.

(why did you put me here)

"Why did you die, you bastard?"

(carol…)

"I'll never forgive you for that. You ruined everything!"

(carol…)

"How could you leave me alone?" Carol wasn't sure if she had shouted it or not; the stifling fog swallowed her echo. The daze fell heavily upon her as she imagined (*or is this happening?*) her body spiraling out of control into the sky. She felt herself alone again for a moment.

"Stu?"

(yes)

"Where are we going?"

(you don't have to worry anymore)

"What'll happen to me?"

(you'll be forgiven)

"Good," she said, and gave into the sleep that she had dreamed of for years.

* * *

Strangely enough, Warren Bennett was the discoverer of the body of Carol Crantz as she sat motionless in Stoneridge Cemetery. He had not wanted to look too closely at the houses anymore, hoping to avoid the type of ordeal he had faced that morning when he discovered the milk bottle on Mrs. Babcock's doorstep. He instead diverted his glance towards the cemetery, knowing it was a safe move as nobody ever went near it. His gaze rested on the woman for only an instant, but it was enough. With a sorry shake from his head, he threw down his empty milk basket and looked pleadingly into the sky. The Ryans were awoken that morning to the shout of, "Why the hell can't I ever get a break around here?"

The officer arriving on the scene muttered the same question to himself as he coughed out the sick aroma that engulfed Parker Street and trudged towards the woman. He jotted down in his notebook that the barefoot woman's skin had begun to turn blue from exposure to the night air, but was unsure if this was connected to the cause of death.

The only fact he felt reluctant to record was the diverted look of peace that lay frozen on a face that seemed strangely acquainted with sorrow. It was almost as if life was reigning in the dead woman's eyes.

INDEPENDENCE DAY

THE GOSPEL ACCORDING TO CLETUS BRUESOME

In my researches into the realm of the inexplicable, there is nothing stranger than the June 28th – July 4th 2008 diary entries of Mr. Cletus Bruesome, age fifty, of Las Cruces, NM. Although the police found many notebooks in his bedroom, this notebook was found lying in the empty bathtub, reasonably undamaged. Although there are many real-life reasons to explain the events detailed in these entries, especially considering Mr. Bruesome's history and state of mind, I find it fascinating that he seemed lucid enough to set down on paper what must have been, at least through his eyes, an unbelievable series of events and I'm left to wonder exactly how much of what happened was actually in his own imagination.

The entries are presented exactly as he wrote them, with all the profanity and racial slurs left in (although most spelling errors have been removed to enhance readability). I sincerely hope that no one will take offense at my decision to present Mr. Bruesome's thoughts in unedited form. - CTO

JUNE 28th, 2008 – That damned nigger's dog came around here barking at six in the morning like always, but that's the last time: its head is sitting on the TV set. It's right next to Old Dud, the dud grenade that my Daddy brought back from the Pacific when it didn't kill him. I put plastic over the back of the set so the blood wouldn't seep back there and short it out. It wasn't a big dog, but it had a shitload of blood in it!

I look at it during the commercials. That keeps me going until the program starts up again. If I'm lucky, its owner will come around here looking for it. Then I'll have two heads to look at.

When Mildred left two days ago, I told her that I would find someone else to replace her, like one of those plastic dummies in the department stores. And now I've got something better than a dummy to keep me company: I've got Man's best friend. Ha! He doesn't have much spunk in him, more the type that just lays around, but Hey; a pal's a pal. Fetch Rover! Ha!

He's got some new friends too: they're small and they came in through the window. What the fuck do I care? The more the merrier; that's what it says in my book!

So I've got my TV, my beer, my case of Jack, my guns, my frozen burgers and fries (no more pansy-ass salads from Mildred), my bowie knife (need to clean it – Rover made a mess of it), my titty-mags, my flies and, most important, I've got Rover – my best friend.

The only thing I really need is an air conditioner. Maybe I'll get myself one for my birthday. On July 4th, I'll be the big 5-0. Fifty and free, that's me. Free as a bird on the Fourth of July, just like the country, and I want to celebrate! My momma told me that she wanted to name me "Indy" because of the day I was born on, but Daddy wouldn't let her, Thank Christ. What kind of sissy name is "Indy" anyway? Only an idiot would be named "Indy". On my fifth birthday, she tried calling me "Indy" just as a joke, but Daddy didn't find it funny at all and let her know it, the way a man has to from time to time, you understand? Well, Mildred never understood, and as she got older and fatter she started hitting back! Hard! Better to just let her go her own way; let her bruise some other chump's arms. I laughed when she stomped out of here, the whole house shaking under her fat feet. I think I heard the floor groan with relief when she left for the last time. But I laughed. Then I got my usual case of PBR and the celebratory case of Jack. Clyde at the liquor store asked me where the party was and I told him "my place, because the hippo's waddled off." I felt so good that I bought him a bottle of Jack. He came by when the store closed; by that time I was pretty far gone, but it was good having him here, carting his half-empty bottle. Drinking on the job, that's Clyde. We whooped it up most of the night and when he passed out in the bathtub, the last thing I heard him talking about was what a lucky guy I was and how he's gonna burn his house down with his family inside and make it look like an accident.

I didn't go to bed: I sat up and watched the sun coming up with the porch spinning all around me. Breathing the cleanest air on God's earth and lolling about in the chair with my head full of Jack was one of the best, most satisfying times of my life. When Clyde woke up after four hours, screaming about his headache and throwing up on the floor, I threw him out. If he wants someone to take care of him, he can find Mildred: she'll take of him, all right. I made him clean up his puke first, of course. And mine (he didn't know the difference; it's not like our names were on it). Why should I get my hands dirty when he's gonna be cleaning up puke anyway? Puke's puke, right? That's what it says in my book.

I went to bed around ten in the morning after fixing myself some bacon and beans. By that time I was losing my buzz and knew it was safe to bed down. I put on some music and went to sleep thinking about how long it's been since I've done exactly what I wanted. I'd called the garage and told Lou that he was in charge for the day because of a family crisis. I think I might have this crisis go on for a while.

Rover looks hungry. He's a good dog and he deserves a bone. I'll dig one of his leg bones out of the trash. A bone's a bone, right? That's what it says in my book.

JUNE 29th, 2008 – Called the garage and expanded on my "family crisis"; I told Lou that my uncle in Tucson was dying in the hospital with cancer. I'm pretty sure he can handle everything. I should have thought of this years ago: just let Lou and his dumbass brother do the work and let the money come in. Of course, the only reason I went in every day was to get away from Mildred. Now the house is just the way I want it, without her moping around and giving me shit about how the TV is gonna turn my brains into "orange marmalade", as she used to say. Why orange marmalade, that's what I want to know. I guess if my brains turned into chucky peanut butter, that would have been alright with her. Lord knows she went through jars of it like pigs go through swill, so I guess that makes sense.

Rover is still enjoying his bone. He's a good dog: never begs from the table or needs to be walked. Faithful to the end, that's my Rover. Although I'm gonna have to do something about his friends; they keep landing on the TV screen and blocking the picture.

Gonna go get a shot of Jack and a beer... or maybe a shot of beer and a glass of Jack. That's sounds like a much better idea.

(Later)

That fucking sow! She went and emptied the bank account! She had no fucking right to do that!

I went down to the liquor store to get a refill on the beer since I was down to seven (I still had more than enough JD) and my bank card came back denied. I couldn't believe it! Even that slimeworm Clyde refused me! I just stood there looking at him and couldn't believe that this was the same guy I'd bought a bottle of JD for and treated to the best time he'd had since he said "I do" to that buck-toothed stringbean of his. I tried to tell him that it was just some stupid bank mistake and just let me take the stuff and I would pay him later, but he wouldn't budge! I lost my temper - anybody would - and I yelled, "Now look, you asshole, we've been friends a long time and I'm not gonna leave here until I get what's coming to me!" And that's when he started slowly bending forward without taking his eyes off me. He was bending to reach under the counter. I knew what that sissy drunk had under there. Before he had a chance to get his hands around it, I pointed my finger at him and yelled, "I won't forget this, you fuck! Just see if I ever come in here again!" He didn't say a word when I left; he just remained crouched with his fingers brushing up against that shotgun. Some friend, that asshole fuckface!

It was no better at the bank. I demanded to see the manager and they sent over some beaner named Senor Hermandoze or something and he started to tell me that since both our names are on the account, Mildred had a perfect right to withdraw the money. I couldn't believe that I was standing there in the middle of that bank while that spic said in broken Engleesh "Oh Seer, I'm teeribly sorry, but de bank it has no responseebeelity in domeestic affairs". Bank of America, my ass; if I had known that a guy like that was in charge I never would have put my money in there. See if I ever drink tequila again. I'll stick to good, old-fashioned, Tennessee whiskey.

I just got his card out of my wallet: Juan Hernandez, that's his name. You just watch the papers: that asshole is a dead man. Now all I've got is a hundred and fifty in poker winnings that I had stashed away and the garage takings. I'm gonna have to call Lou tomorrow to have him bring whatever's in the safe down here. I took some of my winnings down to another liquor store that was a further walk. (Did I mention that the cow took the car too? I should call the cops.) I'm all stocked up for a few days; I even bought a can of bug spray for Rover's buddies. Sprayed a shitload in the living room and loved seeing their little bodies falling to the floor like… well, like flies, I guess. The bug spray smells good, too, although it made me cough at first. I think I'll sleep in the living room tonight, especially since I took a big shit on Mildred's side of the bed just to show her. I like it better in the living room anyway.

JUNE 30th, 2008 – Something incredible happened today. You're gonna think I'm crazy, but I don't care because I'm beyond what all of you think.

I'll start from the beginning. I woke after eleven feeling all out of sorts. The first thing I noticed was puke on the cushion next to my head and I said a quick prayer of thanks that I hadn't choked. I toyed with the idea of calling Clyde and forcing him down here to clean it up, telling him that he'd missed a spot from the other night, but I didn't think that even he, dumbass as he is, would believe that. I stood up and nearly fell right on my face; I'd never felt so dizzy after a night of drinking before. It might have something to do with sleeping in the same room with that bug-killer in the air. When I steadied myself, I saw that more flies had gotten in during the night and they were buzzing all around. I emptied another quarter of the can into the air and the dizziness got stronger; not unpleasant, just stronger. And the smell was great; I just stood in the middle of the room for about ten minutes just taking great big sniffs of the air. It drowns out the puke smell and Rover doesn't seem to mind.

I eventually got my head together and called Lou and told him to bring the money in the safe down. He sounded nervous and stalled by asking me how my uncle was and for a minute I didn't know what the Hell he was talking about. When I figured it out, I came clean and said that I just hadn't felt like coming in, but that I was still his boss and that he'd better bring the money quicker than he could say, "Yes Sir, right away!" But he just sort of stuttered and finally told me what happened.

"Boss, somebody held us up yesterday and got away with most of the day's take."

I nearly crushed the receiver in my hand when I heard that. I asked him to repeat it… twice. Then I asked him what had the day's take been doing sitting in the register when it should have been in the safe. And then stuttering so much that I thought I would be on the phone with that moron for the rest of the day, he told his that his numbnuts brother, Jerry, who'd only been with us a few weeks, decided to keep his head up his ass for most of the day and forgot to drop the cash every hour like he was supposed to do. After ten minutes passed and I finished telling Lou what I was going to do to his brother if I ever saw him wearing a pair of coveralls with my logo on it again, Lou did say that the stick-up guy didn't take a check from old man Jamison for $500. I told him to close up the shop, cash the check, and bring it over before his mother lost two sons instead of just one.

I stomped back into the living room and sat down on the couch to think (avoiding the puke, of course). My bank account was empty, and most of the money that I was counting on was stolen by some punk kid, probably a nigger. All around I was surrounded by idiots and thieves, taking what was mine or just letting others make off with it all. I swore that I wasn't going to let these bastards get away with it! They would get hurt and they would know that it was me that did it.

And the first to get it would be those forchristsakes, Goddamned flies!

I sprayed the repellant all over the room and watched the flies fall, stomping on their tiny corpses as I went. Then I gave myself a good, long spray, felt the tension wearing away, and started to go to the kitchen to crack open the next bottle of JD when I heard it behind me.

"That felt good, didn't it?"

I stopped dead in my tracks. It wasn't a voice that I'd ever heard before, but somehow it felt familiar, like something I'd been waiting for all my life. I turned around, expecting to see someone just magically standing there, but the room was empty: just the dead flies, Old Dud and Rover.

"Up here, Dumbass!"

That's when I noticed that the leg bone had dropped out of Rover's mouth and was laying on the floor. I looked at him and his mouth moved.

"Come over here; I wanna talk to you."

The dog's head, stuck in a mound of dried blood, was talking to me. In fact, I think it was trying to use its head to motion me towards it, which ain't easy when there's nothing below the neck.

"Are you gonna stand there all day, or what?" it asked in a loud voice. It shocked me so much that I was heading for it before I realized I was moving. The dead flies crunched under my feet.

"That's close enough," it said, and I stopped, unable to keep from staring. "Now, I've been watching you for the last few days and there's a few things that we need to discuss."

"Who are you?" I asked, barely moving my mouth.

"What?"

"I… I just wanted to know… I mean… could you talk… before I… I…"

"Before you cut my head off?"

I just nodded dumbly in front of it.

"If I told you I was God, would that shut you up?"

I couldn't believe what I was hearing. "Are you God?"

"Yeah, whatever. Now…"

"Holy shit, I cut off God's head!"

"God commands you to SHUT UP!" It yelled. I shut up.

"First of all, I think that you should know that I don't find what you did with my leg bone amusing. Got that? Now, that that's out of the way, I just wanted to tell you that you're going about this all the wrong way, which is a shame because you've got what it takes to solve all your problems. You understand?"

I nodded.

"No you don't," It said, "but at least you're listening. Take a look at the floor. What do you see?"

I was so shocked by what was happening that I couldn't answer right away.

"God commands you to respond."

"Dead flies."

"Who killed them?"

"I did."

"And you left them on the floor because you wanted to stomp them into paste, right?"

I nodded, not wanting to admit that I simply hadn't given a shit.

"I like that about you, Cletus, enough to put something like cutting my head off behind me… for now." His voice got gruffer right at the end; I got the message.

"What do you want me to do?"

It opened Its mouth the way dogs do when they look like they're smiling at you. "Learn a new word: Trim."

"Trim," I repeated.

"When you're eating baked ham, and there's a lot of fat on it, what do you do to it?"

"Trim it."

"When you've got too much hair, what do you do?"

"Trim it." I was getting the hang of this.

"And when you've got idiots and thieves coming at you from all sides, taking everything that you worked hard for away with just a shrug, what do you do?"

You listen to what God is telling you.

Fifteen minutes later, Lou came by with the money. The door was already unlocked and I told him to come in. I didn't go over to meet him; I just stood in the living room doorway with my left arm hidden from him. I made him walk across the kitchen and hand me the money. Then I told him to get out and when he was half-way to the door, I pulled out the shotgun and fired. It caught him right in the back of the neck, blew his Goddamned head off. I swear I saw him take another step or two before he fell; that asshole had no idea what hit him.

So now I had my money, not a lot, but it would keep me going a while.

I put Lou in the bedroom, on Mildred's side with the shit. The smell in there was so bad that I had to have a few sprays of the bug-killer to get that shit out of my nose.

Oh, I should mention that Lou's head is on the TV now: I don't want God to get lonely.

JULY 1st, 2008 – I was thinking about what I said yesterday to Lou about his mother losing two sons instead of one. Oh, the poor woman.

The two of them drank at Miller's Cave, which is where I waited for the bastard. I had my bowie knife and Daddy's old bayonet with me, rusty but I did some work restoring it so that it could be used again.

To tell the truth, I brought it along in case he caught sight of me: if you saw a man coming at you with a bayonet, rusty or not, you'd drop dead before he had chance to stab you.

He drove into the lot around 2:00 to knock back a few beers (probably that fancy-ass Sam Adams swill). Once he went inside, I slashed the front tire closest to the tree that I'd picked to hide behind and then settled back in my spot. I knew I was in for a long wait, but I didn't care. What else did I have to do today, host the flower show or something? I had a nearly full bottle of Jack with me.

A little more than half a bottle later (about maybe 70 minutes), Jerry came out. I never felt sharper in my life. He did exactly what I wanted him to do: he got in the car, started it up and began to pull out when he felt something wrong on the right side. He got out and walked around to the flat tire. His last words were, "Aw, fuckin' shit." He'll never get into Heaven with that mouth. I probably should have used the bowie knife, but I'd spent all morning on the bayonet and wanted to put it to good use and a blade's a blade, right? That's what it says in my book.

I would've taken his head with me, but a car was pulling into the lot just as he hit the ground. Too bad for Lou: now he won't have anyone to talk to.

Confessed to the Dog that I didn't have time to bring the head back. He didn't say anything. I think He's displeased with me. I asked Him if he wanted me to brush the maggots off Him. He didn't say.

Took a few hits of the spray before going to bed. Didn't bother with the flies; let them get their own!

JULY 2nd, 2008 – Fuck! Who would've thought that pansy-ass, taco-suckin', beaner spic was so tough!

I tried the same plan as yesterday on Mr. Juan "I-shouldn't-even -be-in-this-country-and-I'm-fucking-over-real-Americans" Hernandez. Slashed a tire, hid behind a dumpster, was ready to get him when he came out for lunch. Fuckin' beaner took it in his office. Probably takes a lot of other stuff in his office, right up the ass! I waited all fuckin' day for him to come out and the bottle was nearly empty by the time he did. I forced myself to wait for him to inspect his flat and not just charge out at him, even though it would've been more rewarding to see his tequila-stained eyes when I shoved the bayonet in his gut. I waited, dammit. My head and stomach were fuckin' around with me and I felt like I had to puke, but I kept it down and waited. I heard him start the car, stop it again, and get out and go around to inspect the tire. He was there and he was mine. I jumped up!

And the son-of-a-whore heard me! I must have kicked some rubbish or groaned because I'd been crouching down for hours. But he spun around and hit my arm faster than I could see it happen. The Goddamned bayonet went flying. Daddy's gonna kill me for that!

The bowie was tucked into my belt and I scrabbled for it. I took my eyes off him for just a second and that's when he kicked me right in the balls! The puke that I'd tried to keep down came up anyway. What kind of girlie way is that to fight? If you're gonna fight, fight fair! That's what it says in my book.

I'm sure no one will think any less of me when I say that I dropped the bowie and went down. Fuck, even a marine would go down. He turned tail and ran off shouting for the security guard. I knew I was horsemeat if I hung around so, even with everything inside screaming at me, I managed to straighten up and started moving out of there, fast as I could. Even I was impressed! I just kept running, not lookin' back. I ran down any street or alley that I happened to catch sight off, not caring if I was heading closer to home or not. I heard sirens, but they were far behind me. After twenty minutes, I finally started recognizing where I was and made a beeline home. I didn't hear any sirens and there was nobody waiting for me when I got there; I guess the cocksucker didn't get a good look at my face.

I think I'll set up some chairs in the kitchen tonight; I don't feel right about sleeping in the living room with Him looking at me.

Good thing I left the bug spray on the kitchen table.

JULY 3rd, 2008 – Three a.m. Just woke up. Had the worst fuckin' dream of my life.

For the rest of the day yesterday, I stayed in the kitchen. I ate, drank and sucked up the spray without even going near the living room. I set up a few chairs like I said I would around 11:30 and drank the last quarter of my next-to-last bottle of JD to get to sleep.

Everything was quiet for a while, but then I heard a sound coming from the bedroom. The door opened and I heard slow, shuffling footsteps. Since I was just waking up, I nearly sat up, ready to tell

Mildred to get her fat ass in bed and stop making noise, but the chairs I was sleeping on reminded me that I was alone. I just lay there, trying and failing to see the dark ceiling, and I listened and felt something walk by me. I heard it go into the living room and I breathed a little easier. But then I heard it again, coming back into the kitchen. After a couple of steps on the linoleum, it got quiet again. My head was still spinning from the Jack and I was trying to hear something in the dark, anything, especially breathing. Finally, there was a new sound: buzzing.

Since my eyes were now used to the dark, I looked towards the living room door. There was Lou, struggling to keep his balance and to keep his head, which he had gone to the living room to fetch, from falling off his shoulders. It squelched and jiggled unsteadily and I knew I'd run screaming into the night if I saw it fall off while the rest of his body kept standing. After two days, he was already turning to shit, but that didn't stop him from standing there with his finger pointing right at me. And the buzzing got louder. Then through the door came a tight swarm of flies, carrying the Dog's head. It dipped and bobbed in the air and the flies readjusted to hold Him up properly. Although it was tough to see at first, they brought Him closer and I could finally make out the thing that He held in His mouth: Old Dud. The swarm followed Lou's pointing finger and carried the Head and Old Dud until they were floating right over me. That close, I saw something that I had never noticed before: Old Dud's handle had never sprung; it was still locked against the side of the grenade. That's why it didn't kill Daddy and sat on shelves and TV sets for sixty-four years without exploding; it wasn't because the fuse was faulty or the charges got wet: the handle just hadn't sprung.

For the first time, I began to wonder if that handle was permanently jammed or if it had just been waiting for the right moment.

And when the Dog's head opened Its mouth, I knew that Old Dud had picked its moment.

I rolled off the chairs and hit the floor with a slam that nearly knocked me out. I put my hands over my head and waited for the blast. Nothing happened. When I finally looked up, Lou, the flies, the Head and Old Dud were gone, like they'd never been there.

I'm gonna sleep in the bathtub; there's a lock on the bathroom door.

JULY 3rd, 2008 (evening) – First thing in the morning, I peeked into the living room to see if they were all still in there and they were: the Dog, Lou, the flies, all there. I didn't want any of them to see me so I didn't stay long.

I know the Dog is upset because I didn't take care of that asshole from the bank. If last night was anything to go by, I've got to do something to satisfy Him before He decides to pick up Old Dud for real. I knew I couldn't go back to the bank; they'd be on the lookout for me. I sat at the table thinking for a while, taking a few pulls on the last bottle of Jack and scooping up a few forkfuls of godawful beans that were left over from days ago, and I finally thought of Clyde, that ass-lickin' pussy-whipped faggot who thought he was so big with his shotgun and everything after I'd shown him a good time. Yeah, Clyde would be a good one to visit next, I thought, especially since it'd been a few days since he'd seen me and he wouldn't be expecting it. I'd lost my knives at the bank, but I still had my guns in the house. I knew I'd have to do it soon before the police started putting two and two together about Lou and his asshole brother.

Just then, the phone rang. I answered it with a friendly "What?"

"Cletus, it's me Mildred."

Clyde's guardian angels must have been working overtime.

"Where are you?"

"I don't think I should tell you that."

"Then what did you call for?"

I could tell that she was thinking about hanging up and I decided to play it cooler. "I'm sorry," I said, "but things haven't been going well. Somebody ripped off the garage and now Lou's disappeared. I think he had something to do with it."

"Cletus, I want to meet with you… with my lawyer."

With every word she said, I knew that it was gonna be more and more fun to take care of her. "You got a lawyer, now?"

"I think it's for the best. I'm not coming back and we need to end things as cleanly as we can."

Oh, it'll be clean, I thought.

"I don't want to take anything that's yours."

Yeah, except all my money, ya' lyin' bitch.

"Yeah, I know," I lied. "Why don't you and your lawyer come down here and we'll talk turkey?"

She didn't answer for a minute and she said, "I don't think that's a good idea."

She'd begun to get this sixth sense about things in the last few years: whenever I was creeping up on her, quiet as a mouse, ready to teach her a lesson, she'd always know I was there and spring up and get me first. The damned thing must've been ringing bells in her head.

"Do you think we could meet at Charlie's Diner tomorrow evening?" she asked.

"Taking me out for my birthday, huh?"

We fixed the time for seven in the evening and I hung up. Charlie's Diner was a great idea on her part; the cops were gonna catch up with me soon enough and if it was Mildred's time to go, why should she go all by herself like Lou did? The more the merrier; that's what it says in my book.

And it would be the 4th of July: nobody would notice one more firework going off.

I took the last hit from the can to celebrate and felt the world turn 'round. Then I heard the voice from the next room: "DO IT RIGHT THIS TIME, SHITHEAD!"

Later, I went out and got more JD and more bug spray. When I was walking home, I saw a homemade poster on a tree with a picture of a lost dog on it. I tore it down, took it home and wiped my ass with it.

I'm gonna sleep in the bathroom again tonight.

JULY 4th, 2008 – Happy Birthday, America! Happy Birthday, Cletus! So now you're fifty! How does it feel?

Free, just like it should be on the 4th. Today, I will earn my freedom.

I'm taking a big tote bag with me to Charlie's – it's only got two things in it: a full gas can and a grill lighter. There's gonna be some fireworks tonight!

(Later)

I'm fucked.

Happy Birthday, Indy. So now you're fucked. How does it feel?

I was sitting there in Charlie's, with my bag at my side on the floor, drinking down the double Jack that I'd ordered, keeping my eye on the window for Mildred. I was sitting right there at the window, just staring out, looking for her. I knew people in the diner were looking at me, what with me not having showered in a little while and all, and I guess the look in my eye might have put a few people off, but I didn't care. I was ready for the celebration: Hell, who isn't once the sun goes down on the 4th.

I saw her and her lawyer – her COON lawyer – crossing the street and I realized the truth. The punk who ripped off the garage was related to that guy. It was all a setup, planned by Mildred, to take every fuckin' thing she could get her fat hands on: if my dick came off, she'd be tryin' to get that too! She was probably fucking him too… and the punk! I saw it as clear as day: my wife in a three-way in a hotel in Jamaica or some fuckin' place where all the men run around with their dicks swinging free, paid for with my money! I put my hand on the window, wanting to reach through it and strangle her until she turned green and puked her big fat stomach into the street!

That must have been what set her off; she stopped dead in the middle of the street, stopping the coon with her, and I could see from her face that she'd figured it out. That damned sixth sense of hers had just started blaring away in her head. I could see that the coon looked concerned, but Mildred pulled him back to the other side of the street before the lights changed again. Through it all, I kept whispering "No, no, no, no" as I watched her talking frantically to him, trying to convince him that they should get the Hell out of there before the shit hit the fan.

He didn't look like he was gonna stand up to her arguments for long (some fuckin' lawyer). I knew it was my last chance.

I jumped up with my bag and ran out the door, trying to unzip the damned thing and get the cap on the can open. I collided with two people on the sidewalk and kept going. I'd gotten the cap off and gas splashed on me and people could see what I was up to. Mildred saw me and screamed. I tried to run across the street, but the cars wouldn't let me through. They honked as they went by and I kicked at one and screamed at it. Gas was spilling all over me and on the street. The coon started to hustle her off and I screamed as loud as I could over the city noise, "Come back here, you fuckin' whore! Nigger-Fucker! It's my birthday, remember? Let's light the cake! Fuck you! Come back here and take what's coming to ya'!"

When I looked around, I saw that people had cleared away from me; even the cars were giving me space. And there were eyes, hundreds of them it seemed like, all of them looking and remembering my face. I had an urge to use the grill lighter, what with me covered in gas, and just let them look at the maniac as he went up in front of them.

But it's my birthday, and that's no way to celebrate being fifty. Instead, I ran.

When I got home, there was a phone message from Mildred, telling me that she would give me time to turn myself in either to the police or the loony bin, but that she was gonna make the call tomorrow morning if I hadn't done it by then. The Dog must've heard that; the phone is right next to the living room door. It knows what happened.

I looked into the living room and It had Old Dud in Its mouth.

I've locked myself in the bathroom, with the gas can and the grill lighter. I'm ready: if I hear the buzzing coming closer, I think I can throw the gas on It and use the grill lighter before It has time to drop Old Dud. And even if I can't, I can't stay in here forever; the cops will be here soon and they'll find Lou.

I've also got the bug spray in here with me. I probably shouldn't be dosing right now, what with Old Dud out there somewhere, but it's my birthday and I deserve to be happy, right? That's what it says in my book.

I think I hear something out there. Just a minute, I'm gonna check.

(Entry ends here)

Interestingly enough, a Mr. Ned Johnson was wandering close to Mr. Bruesome's house, looking for his dog which had gone missing the week before, when he heard the explosion. He claims that, at first, he didn't attach any significance to it because he'd been hearing explosions all night. "After all," he told the police, "it was the 4th of July, wasn't it?"

ST. SWITHUN'S DAY

SORRY, COULDN'T THINK OF ANYTHING

Dear Ray,

I'm afraid that your idea of a story based on "St. Swithun's Day" was, in a ~~manner~~ manner of speaking, Crap!

As these pages should prove, I couldn't think of anything. No one's ever <u>heard</u> of it anyway!

Let's just go from "Cletus" to "Gloomiest!"

Thanx CTO

P.S. – I must stress that these pages are <u>not</u> my idea for a St. Swithun's story. I really couldn't think of anything. Do <u>not</u> put these in the book!

LABOR DAY

THE GLOOMIEST OF MEN

"Executions were now a stimulus to his fury, and he ordered the death of all who were lying in prison under accusation of complicity with Sejanus. There lay, singly or in heaps, the unnumbered dead, of every age and sex, the illustrious with the obscure. Kinsfolk and friends were not allowed to be near them, to weep over them, or even to gaze on them too long… The force of terror had utterly extinguished the sense of human fellowship, and, with the growth of cruelty, pity was thrust aside." – *The Annals Of Tacitus.*

* * *

Labor Day Weekend… God's gift to the man who lives within driving distance of Vegas…

So mused Jake Hannay as he cruised back to Los Angeles along route 604, not his usual route but it was Labor Day and he had all the time in the world to explore a new route and get back home in time to see Jerry Lewis sing his last song of the telethon, make himself a hamburger and a tall, cold tequila and lime so he could prepare properly for his return to his academic duties at USC. Just the thought of facing that first class of deadheads without at least the shred of a hangover made him shiver: he'd taught some morons in his time, but he thought that this group must've made a blood-pact of stupidity. How they could make it to college-level History and think that Ulysses Grant was "the guy who sailed off to find the golden fleas", as one would-be brain surgeon told him, was completely beyond him. Still, that headache was for tomorrow; today's headache would come out of a tequila bottle and he was looking forward to it, especially since Mandy was in England and wouldn't be back until Friday. But first there was route 604 to the city of Jean to contend with and, after that, civilization.

The road was quiet, only the occasional car passed him on the other side and there was nothing in his mirrors. It was still early: he'd left the hotel immediately after breakfast, surprising the hotel staff who couldn't believe that a guest would leave so early on a holiday. But he'd partied as hearty as he wanted to and now he was ready for quiet-decompression-in-front-of-the-tube time. Jake stole a few glances at the scenery around him: train tracks running along his right side a short distance away and nothing but dirt, land and hills on his left. With the windows open and his hair blowing, Jake didn't mind that he could barely hear the Rolling Stones CD that he'd loaded up; to sniff the sharp wind was to feel power and awareness in his head and down his back. He slowed slightly to take in another relaxing glance at the scenery.

A horn blared and something shot around him from behind and accelerated ahead, leaving fumes mixed in with what was once breathable air. Jake nearly slammed on the brakes. He squinted and, even though it was now forty feet in front of him, he could make out "1V7-SFW" on the California plate attached to the red roadster. Jake gritted his teeth and made a snap decision, without realizing that he'd done it, to not let the speeder out of his sight. He thumped the accelerator and, although the old car resisted for a moment, Jake steadily started gaining on the speeder.

"Jesus, look at that nut go," he muttered as he struggled to get closer than sixty feet to the roadster's tail. Whoever the driver was, he'd obviously decided to stretch his engine's muscles on the mostly empty road and woe betide the possum that scuttled in front of him. The roadster put on an extra burst of speed and Jake was amazed that it was now about ninety feet ahead, scorching the road. Jake shook his head in disbelief, knowing it was fruitless to attempt to keep on the roadster's tail and was just about to slow down when something happened in front of him that made him gasp.

Though quite small in his windshield because of the distance, Jake saw the roadster swerve slightly as if it were about to lose control and, in almost the same moment, something went flying from the road into the small gully running along the side. Even at a distance, Jake knew that it was a man who'd gone flying and was probably dead the second he hit the gully. Without checking his mirror, Jake slammed on the brakes, not believing that he'd really witnessed what just happened. Suddenly remembering where he was, he checked his mirrors to make sure he wasn't about to get rear-ended by some poor soul who wouldn't be able to stop in time. Thankfully, the road behind him was clear. Jake sat quietly for a minute, listening to his heart beating heavily, staring at the now-empty road ahead of him: the roadster never even slowed down.

"What the Hell am I doing?" he gasped and drove forward, slowing down at where he guessed the accident occurred. He craned his neck, peering out of the right-hand window and crept along until he saw the unmistakable evidence of the roadster's recklessness. He stopped and got out of the car, half-running to the body laying in the gully. He didn't even realize that he'd stomped on an already-shattered pair of glasses until much later.

It was a man in his sixties with long white hair and a beard. His face was burnt red and cracked from the sun and the cancerous sores on his face and hands told him that the man had been traveling in the sun for a long time. He was dressed in ripped blue jeans (torn from the accident, if the blood was anything to go by), a Grateful Dead t-shirt and a jeans jacket, which bulged at his side in a way that suggested that some ribs had been broken. Around his forehead was a dirty blue bandana, bleached light from the sun with one round dark spot in the center, as if it were hiding a wound in his forehead.

Jake slowed up, saving himself from losing his balance on the steep incline. He crept up on the body, never having seen a corpse before, and felt his head swim. Everywhere the man's clothes were torn, there was blood; even the man's mouth was bloody from his broken front teeth. He was laying at an angle that could only mean that the back had broken on impact. It was only the sound of a gurgling cough, of the man spitting out the blood that he was choking on, that brought Jake back to the crisis.

My God, he's still alive!

Jake hurriedly made his way beside the man, being careful not to touch him in the slightest, and crouched next to his head. The man strained to lift his head, but Jake placed his hand gently on the man's forehead.

"Please don't move, Mister."

The man was struggling to breathe and Jake couldn't bring

himself to say something like, "don't worry; you're going to be okay". If the man was aware of anything, he must have been aware that the clear sky above was the last thing he was ever going to see.

The man spit out more blood and he said between heavy breaths, "So... finally it, huh?"

Jake found himself tongue-tied and jabbered the first thing that came to his head. "I saw what happened! That guy didn't even slow down! I got his license plate. He won't get away with this."

The man raised his eyes to look into Jake's. "...wasn't you?"

"It was this red sports car that tore past me a ways back. I don't know what the Hell was wrong with him." When the man shut his eyes tightly, as if in complete frustration, Jake took a deep breath and tried to keep him talking. "What's your name, Mister?"

With great effort, he groaned, "Pigpen... like in... Charlie Brown."

Jake took a moment to make sure that he'd heard right. "Pigpen, okay. Listen, Pigpen, I can't lie to you; you're hurt really bad and there's nothing I can..."

Pigpen took another deep breath. "You've got to..."

"I'm sorry, but you can't be moved."

"You've got to get out of here, kid... before..."

Pigpen lost his wind at that point and struggled to speak again. Jake tried to silence him. "Look, I'm not going to leave you alone out here. I may not be able to do any good, but I can't just take off and leave you..."

"...gotta' go. You'll be... taken..."

"Save your strength, Man."

But then Pigpen's voice got very low as he concentrated every last ounce of strength in what he had to say.

"I'm the Zodiac Killer!"

A seizure shook Pigpen's head and thumped it into the ground. A choking gasp escaped out of him and his body froze into a rigid knot of pain for a moment before he slumped into the dirt with one last bubble of blood spurting from his flaccid lips.

Jake, crouched beside Pigpen's now-dead body, fell backwards and sat in the dirt. Every nerve under his skin was alert and itching; a few inches from his feet lay a dead man who, in his last breath, confessed to being the most notorious and slippery serial killer since Jack The Ripper. He stared harder, trying to force himself to believe it and couldn't; it was a dirty drifter in dirty clothes who'd drifted too far into the path of the wrong car, just a simple bum in jeans, t-shirt and bandana.

Jake noticed that the bandana had slipped over the dead man's eyes during his final seizure and his forehead was exposed. In the center of his forehead was the wound that Jake had guessed would be there: a deep and bloody cross within a circle carved into the flesh that had probably only stopped bleeding when the man's heart had stopped beating. His natural memory for history was jolted by the symbol: it was the symbol that had been signed on notes written by The Zodiac Killer.

He couldn't bear to look at the dead man any longer so he stared at a distant passing train. Vaguely, he wondered how he had gotten into the gully in the first place, sitting inches away from a corpse. With a sad shake of the head, Jake looked back down at Pigpen's body.

The body was gone.

Jake stared in front of him for another minute, but nothing could induce the broken corpse to return to where it should have been. And yet the body had indeed been there because Pigpen's bloodstained clothes were lying rumpled where he had been, from his boots to the bandana, in a vague humanoid shape. Now that the body was gone, Jake could see something sticking out of the jacket's inner pocket: an ivory handle. He grasped it and found himself raising a small machete into the sunlight, the blade coated with dried blood, but still sharp.

Jake's jaw shuddered as he held the blade up and remembered Pigpen's last words. He might have dismissed them as the last flight of a delirious mind, but the blood convinced him: old, dull and flaking, the man had left it to stain his blade, as a sick memento.

But the Zodiac Killer, thought Jake; he was killing in the sixties. He couldn't still be alive.

He isn't, Dumbo; he just dropped dead right in front of you.

A bit dizzy from the sun, Jake dropped his gaze and noticed for the first time something else lying in the folds of the jacket: a scabbard for the blade. When he picked it up, he saw a folded piece of paper sticking out of the top of it. He unfolded the paper and read what was written on it.

"Take the weapon and follow the signs. Sorry."

Jake read the note again and again, trying to make sense of it, and would have sat there for the rest of the day if a drop of blood hadn't dripped and spattered on the word "weapon". He stopped breathing for a moment and brought a hand to his forehead; it came back with blood on two fingers. He forced his trembling fingers to trace the wound on his forehead.

A cross within a circle.

* * *

The girl's name was Jenny and she was nineteen years-old. To look at her was to realize that this was not a girl who'd been living on the road for very long: the backpack she was lugging was only half-full as she'd packed in a hurry to get away from the drunken father who had recently stopped looking at her in a strange way and started using his hands to tell her how he felt about her. She had no hat to protect her from the sun and, if she'd had even a full minute to think about it, she never would have embarked on her journey with nothing more durable on her feet than an old pair of deer-skin moccasins. After four hours of walking, there was a hole worn through the sole of one of them and she thought that her foot would go the same way if she did not find a ride soon. She walked backwards slowly along the soft shoulder of route 604 with her thumb out for a ride and ready to collapse when she saw, off in the distance, a car approaching.

"Oh, Thank God," she said. Although not a hitchhiker by nature, Jenny decided that she would've accepted a ride from Charles Manson if he promised to let her rest her feet for a while with the air conditioner on full blast before he murdered her.

The car finally arrived and slowed down in front of her. The driver leaned over and opened the door for her.

"Hey, thanks," she shouted tiredly, throwing her pack into the back seat and plopping down in the front. "I thought I was gonna die out there!" She closed the door and looked at her new traveling companion: he was in his mid-thirties and dressed casually in clean clothes; she could not see the dust or spots of blood on his pant legs from kneeling in the dirt next to a dying drifter. The only odd thing was the dirty and bleached blue bandana that was tied around his forehead. He looked tired and slightly dazed but otherwise alright, in fact, not bad-looking for an older guy.

"My name's Jenny McCale," she said, "and I'm trying to get to L.A. Are you going anywhere near there, Mister..."

"Hannay, Jake Hannay. I've been trying to get there myself."

"I really appreciate this," she said. She adjusted her seat back, slipped her feet out of her shoes and rested them on the dashboard. "I thought I was gonna walk until they were worn down to the ankles."

Jake didn't respond. He just put the car in gear and started driving down the road, trying to put out of his mind the question of why, after six hours, he was still in Nevada.

"So, what do you do, Mr. Hannah?"

"Hannay. I taught History at USC."

"You don't do it anymore?"

Jake fell into silence for a moment, wondering why he had been compelled to say that. "You have any relations in L.A.?"

"Just trying to get as far away from this patch of Sinai as possible."

For the first time since before a red roadster had sped past him that morning, Jake laughed.

"What's funny?" she asked.

"I was just thinking, if I mentioned Sinai to any of my third-year students, they would probably think I was talking about the hospital. It's nice to meet a young person who knows something she didn't see on 'Hannah Montana'."

Jenny laughed with him. "That's what my mother used to call this area. She was religious. Damn, I'm getting a blister!"

Jenny pulled her dusty foot closer to her face to inspect it and Jake wished that he could just open the door and kick the young, lithe, flexible thing back out into Sinai where she came from. It would be for her own good because...

...blood is sweet...

"Does your mother know that you're out hitchhiking?"

Jenny sighed. "Only if there's a window in Hell pointing up."

"I'm sorry."

She rolled her eyes. "Thanks, but it happened years ago. Besides, when she died, I finally got to go to a real school since Dad had no interest in teaching me. That was fine with me because all of Momma's lessons came out of the Bible."

"And you still think that she's... gone to..."

"Oh yeah, no doubt. Whoever wrote the damn thing forgot to put stuff in Exodus like 'Thou shalt not beat your daughter for growing tits' or 'Thou shalt not shoot thyself up before the children are fed'. Hey, that can't be right!"

They were passing a sign that said "Jean, 50 Miles". Just beyond it was another sign that simply read "Turn Right" without saying what lay in that direction. They passed both signs and the turnoff without Jenny noticing Jake's trembling jaw.

"There was no way I was more than twenty miles from Jean and I was probably closer to ten; I know, I got the sore feet to prove it. What retard put that thing up?"

"Hitchhiking's dangerous, you know," said Jake, ignoring her question. "You've got to be careful out here."

Jenny huffed and continued rubbing her foot. "Why, planning on killing me or something?"

"Don't be silly," he said. Something inside of him growled. "It's just you need to be careful. There are a lot of creeps in the world."

"Yeah, and I've grown up with the worst of them. Trust me; I can spot the creeps in a second. You think I would've gotten into the car with you if you were Jeffrey Dahmer or The Wandering Jew? I can tell just by looking at you that you're okay, although I'd lose that kerchief on your head: that looks a little weird if you don't mind me…"

"The wandering *what*?" Jake thought he knew what she was talking about, but it had been years since he'd heard the reference.

"It's just some stupid story," said Jenny. "Momma hated Jews and she found stuff in the Bible to back her up, like everybody does, you know? Anyway there was one story about a guy who hit Jesus or something and Jesus told him that he would walk the earth until the end of the world. And Momma added her own stuff saying that he was the reason AIDS started up and stuff like that. She always said that it was the Jews fault that Jesus got killed, but I always thought that guy who washed his hands was the real one who did it."

"Pilate," said Jake in a voice that sounded like he was trying to hold something back. "Pontius Pilate. He didn't really want to execute Jesus, but the crowd threatened to report him to…"

"Yeah, I know," said Jenny. "Julius Caesar."

"Tiberius," he corrected. "It was Tiberius Caesar."

"Whatever. Anyway, Momma just wanted to keep me away from Jews because she said…"

Words were spilling into his head in a voice that he'd never heard before; in a language that he didn't speak yet somehow understood.

"…Jewish kids at school were nothing like what Momma said. They were…"

…Eternus Peregrinus… The Eternal Wanderer…

"…one of them was really cute, but when Daddy found out…"

…Operor quis ego dico vos… Do what I tell you…

"…said they were all wrong because they had 'the Mark of Cain' on them or something stupid like that."

"The Mark of what?" Jake asked, knowing what it was but talking in the hope of drowning out the voice.

"The Mark of Cain," she said, giggling. "It's stupid, but she said that when God cursed Cain for killing his brother, He made him an outcast by putting this mark on his…"

Her smile froze on her face as her finger likewise halted on the way to her forehead. Jenny slowly turned to Jake and looked at the bandana wrapped around his forehead. For the first time, she noticed that it looked damp and she could almost see the tiniest trickle of what could be blood seeping from beneath it.

Her silence distracted him from the voice in his head momentarily and he looked at her. "What? What's wrong?"

Jenny eyed him and sat back, closer to the door. "Did you have an accident?"

Jake reached up and touched his forehead, feeling his face turn red when his fingers came back with a trace of blood. "I… fell down."

Jenny stared ahead, not sure what to say next considering that she felt as if she'd just slipped backwards down a tall slide that dumped her back at the age of six when all of her mother's devout bigotry seemed as real as the shadow-ghosts cast by the moonlight when the bedroom lights went out.

"My girlfriend is Jewish," Jake said.

Jenny wasn't sure why he said that, but she decided to play along. "I hope I didn't say anything to offend you or anything. I was just telling you things my mother said to me when I was…"

"…and I'm never going to see her again."

For the first time, Jenny wondered if creeps didn't come in different shapes and sizes from the ones that she'd grown up with. She tucked her feet under her and gripped her ankles, feeling her muscles tense up.

"Why do you say that?"

Jake answered by pointing ahead. Jenny looked and to her surprise she saw the same sign that they had passed not ten minutes before: JEAN, 50 MILES. About thirty yards beyond, she could see the turnoff and the sign reading "Turn Right" looming.

Insisto subcribo…

The voice wanted him to follow the sign.

"But… we just passed that!" she said. "We can't *still* be fifty miles from Jean."

"We *are* still fifty miles from Jean."

"Are we going in circles or something?"

"No," he said as he continued past the signs. "I've been driving straight for hours now."

"But…"

"I've passed those signs thirty-six times."

She snorted despite herself. "Oh, come on! You think I'm a kid or something? You're just *lost* or someth…"

And there, sixty yards away, were the two signs and the turnoff yet again.

"Let me out."

Insisto subcribo…

"I said stop this thing and let me out right now!"

Lavo In Suus Cruor!

It wanted to bathe in her blood. As nausea passed over him, Jake fell back and the other took control.

"Jesus Christ! Let me out of this…!"

And a monster's face turned and grinned hungrily at the frightened girl as he swerved the car onto the dirt road, nearly flipping the car over in the process. Jenny felt her end of the car lifting off the ground and she screamed. She and the right side of the car landed with a thud and she sat dazed as the madman stomped the accelerator as far as it would go.

The road didn't go far, but the car sped into the barren land, kicking up the dust and dirt as it went. Jenny saw the hill supporting the distant train tracks getting closer and she screamed, hugging her head and pressing her feet against the dashboard to brace herself.

Suddenly, the madman swerved to the right and hit the brake, throwing Jenny into him. His right arm locked around her chest and she was pulled out of the car before it came to a stop. The madman dragged her over the dirt, her heels uselessly digging in the dirt in an effort to get away, and she screamed and flailed her arms to hit him. Every strike she landed felt as if she were hitting stone.

"NO! LEAVE ME ALONE! NO! NO! NO!"

He flung her to the ground and she lay there for a moment, trying to get the wind back into her lungs. She slowly lifted her head and knew that she was dead: standing over her was a different man from the one who'd picked her up. He had the same face but it was still different: the lunacy in his eyes had turned them nearly as red as fire and his trembling smile dripped saliva into the dirt. The change in his countenance was so striking that it took her a second to see the small, blood-encrusted machete that he was now wielding.

Oh my God, she thought... It's Cain!

He raised the machete and opened his mouth as if to roar. She covered her head and whimpered.

Ten seconds later, she breathed and realized that she was still alive.

Afraid to make a sound, Jenny gingerly lifted her head, expecting to see the blade slicing down into her. The madman was still standing over her, but with the machete lowered to his side. He was looking off into the distance. She followed his look but could see nothing more than the car twenty feet away. She looked back to the madman; his gaze had not wavered. She gently lifted herself a few inches off the ground, testing his attention. He never looked at her.

Taking a deep breath, Jenny sprang up and started running away, heading for the 604 in the distance. She screamed as she ran, fully expecting footsteps to catch up with her and the sharp shock of the blade. She didn't see the man dressed in robes right in front of her and ran straight through him. His image rippled, but she never noticed it. Still screaming, her strong legs pumped harder and harder until she was a tiny retreating image to the madman. He barely noticed any of this, seeing only the tanned, robed and bearded man calmly approaching.

"Tristissimus Hominum," the robed man said and Jake, buried deep within the mind of the madman and struggling to break free, understood the words clearly.

...*The Gloomiest of Men... the words that Pliney The Elder used to describe...*

"Tiberius," said the robed man in a sad and gentle voice, "must you persist?"

Jake heard the madman speaking to the other in his own voice. "I would have covered myself in her blood. Just as I've done millions of times before. So many times... you have no idea..."

"I know exactly what you have done, starting with the mass executions that you ordered near the end of your reign."

"Conspirers, all of them," the madman spat, "all of them in league with Sejanus to depose me! A man has a right to protect what is his!"

The robed man shook his head sadly. "All that blood to protect a throne you had all but given up voluntarily to Sejanus in the first place?"

"Execution is the only form of punishment that a conspirator understands. Filthy campaigners of plots and secrets, just like you! Pilate told me of you when he returned from Jerusalem. He knew I would have forced him to drink his own blood if he had let even a single conspirator against Rome go unpunished!"

"To this day, you still believe that?" The robed man tried to move closer, but the madman stepped backwards, wielding the blade even though he knew it would do no good. "How long will you shed innocent blood?"

The madman growled his response. "Until you set me free of this curse you've placed on me! Until you let me fly into the arms of the Gods."

"I've done nothing. My Father..."

"I won't listen!" screamed the madman, turning away.

"My Father has rendered unto Caesar what is Caesar's. It is His will."

He turned back to the robed man and advanced, but the robed man was not afraid. "I'll kill more, just as I have before as the Ripper and the Zodiac and with many other faces and names! Think of the lives you could save... remember the old couple I axed a hundred years ago and blamed on their simpleminded daughter, the Short woman in the big city to the west that I chopped in half, the pretty little girls whose families have no peace because their children's bodies molder in their hidden graves... just the beginning... the oceans will turn red..."

But the robed man had already turned and started walking back to where he came from. The madman screamed inarticulate rage at him and, lost as he was for words, Jake found a crack through which he crawled up into his own mouth.

"Sir?" he called out.

The robed man paused.

Frightened that he would be left alone with the madman, Jake tried again. "Lord?"

The robed man turned back, slowly approached Jake and hugged him tightly. Jake felt as if, for just one moment, he was lying at the heart of the greatest tranquility in the universe. The feeling left him when the robed man let him go.

"You must not go home; it is too dangerous for your loved ones. He would kill them without you even knowing."

"But..."

"You must travel, steer clear from what is familiar and find a new way. It will not be easy. Try to resist his influence, if you can, but remember that the sin is his, not yours."

Jake grew afraid at what he was hearing. "This can't be happening. I have a girlfriend, a class of dimwits that I have to teach. I would be there right now if it weren't a holiday. I shouldn't be here! I should be…"

"I'm sorry, my son," the robed man said and rested his hands on Jake's shoulders. "It must be this way. But know that the man whom you comforted…"

"Pigpen?"

"He sits in Paradise at this moment, as you will one day, for the suffering you must endure."

Jake wanted to beg and plead for the man to take it all back or to wave his hands and make it all better as he believed he could, but no words came out. A few tears came to his eyes as he watched the man walk away into the distance and get fainter.

He almost didn't notice the police car speeding up to him and stop twenty yards from his own car until it drove through the robed man's image, which rippled and disappeared. Two large cops jumped out and drew their weapons.

"Drop the knife and get down on the ground, buddy!"

From within the car, Jake could hear Jenny shouting, "That's him! I told you! He's crazy!" The cops kept shouting for him to surrender his weapon and come quietly. The guns, locked in their fat sweaty hands, were inching towards him. And all the noise they were making was inside his head…

And inside the madman's head…

Jake was ready to spring forward into the paths of their bullets, praying he'd be dead before he hit the ground, but in a moment of fear, the madman pushed him aside.

"Don't get too close to him," Jenny shouted from the car. "He's crazy!"

"Not one more step, asshole!"

Jake opened his eyes and found himself sitting at the wheel of his own car, the noise from all the shouting voices snuffed into silence. The first thing he noticed was that the sun had dipped lower in the sky. He frantically patted his chest to feel the bullet holes that he knew must be there, but he was unharmed. The light from the low sun was shining in his eyes and as he turned away, he caught a glimpse of Jenny's discarded old moccasins lying askew on the passenger-side floor. He looked in the backseat and saw her backpack; her clothes were scattered all over from the sudden stop the madman had made. Through the windows, he could see that he was alone except for the police car sitting silently on its own. There were no people anywhere in the vicinity.

No one, he thought. This is the way it's going to be. Why couldn't I have been in class today with those morons?

It was a holiday weekend and he had wanted to get out of town. It could have happened to anyone.

Jake opened the car door and saw two sets of bare footprints heading back to route 604 and guessed that they both belonged to Jenny: she'd made the first set when she first got away from him and the second set after he'd blacked out, apparently.

"She's gone," he muttered. "Thank God."

But then he caught sight of the thing, covered in swarming flies, lying midway between himself and the police car. His breath stopped and he looked closer through the police car's flaring windshield and could just make out two people sitting in the front seats, not moving.

Jake approached the object on the ground and shooed the flies away so he could get a better look at what they were feasting on.

It was a large, bloodstained gun with two fat, disembodied hands still wrapped around it.

HALLOWEEN

GIVE US SOMETHING GOOD TO EAT

Belinda Melcher couldn't stop smiling; it was her favorite night of the year. And although there were adults her own age who complained that Halloween was the stupidest holiday of the year, what with having to continually answer the door and pass out candy to strange children so they could get fat, lose their teeth and start their way down the path to early-onset diabetes because if you didn't you'd find your house covered with smashed eggs in the morning, Belinda couldn't have disagreed more. It had nothing to do with glorious childhood memories of her own (although she had plenty of those) or some perverse need to set up loud, scary noises on a speaker by the front door to frighten approaching children, as she knew some people did. Belinda believed, in fact, that no child or adult on Earth could truly appreciate and enjoy Halloween who didn't live in Beverly Hills, surrounded by people who worked in the movies. Nobody from Concord, Maine to San Diego could possibly experience All Soul's Night the way she experienced it.

Every time the doorbell rang, she skipped with giddy anticipation to the front door and held her breath for a moment before opening it, wondering what vision or glorious monstrosity would be standing on her doorstep. That was one of the special pleasures that she came to look forward to ever since her husband Hal had gotten a five-picture deal at Paramount and could afford to move them to their latest home six years before: the children of industry workers all had connections to makeup artists and costume designers. There was no need for store-bought costumes in any of the surrounding neighborhoods: as Halloween approached, phone calls were made to the specialists who were the best friends of the children's parents. Everyone was happy to work their special and rather expensive magic for free if it made the whole night more entertaining for everyone, especially the children. Belinda even mused that she herself was getting off pretty easy, only providing candy for the kids when most of them had sat in professional makeup chairs like actors do in preparation for the yearly sunset creep. The whole thing simply fascinated her.

What was best was the children who had gone one step further in their holiday plans: while some kids came in twos or threes dressed in whatever they individually desired (one small group had been a vampire, a character from *X-Men* and Fidel Castro), many kids had gotten together and decided to go out as a themed group. So far, Belinda had been graced with visits from *The Dark Knight* characters (Batman, The Joker, The Scarecrow and Ra's al Ghul, who was actually in the first movie but what was the point of quibbling), the traditional Universal monsters and a pack of ten who were dressed as the different doctors from *Doctor Who;* all of this wonderment for the price of a bag of Snickers and jawbreakers. It was better than the late-night Creature Feature.

At ten minutes past nine, twenty minutes since the last visit (what Belinda thought would be the *very* last visit of the night), the doorbell rang and Belinda was a bit surprised to hear it; she'd already taken the bowls of remaining candy back to the kitchen and had just been settling down with a Robert Bloch story, something she did every Halloween. Something inside her told her that this visit wasn't entirely normal; no child had ever come to the door past nine during her time in the neighborhood and she vaguely wondered if it would be the wise choice to simply pretend that she wasn't home, especially since Hal was in New York. She tiptoed to the door and, while the visitors did not try to ring the bell a second time, she heard shuffling and muttered voices on the other side.

"Who is it?"

"Trick-or-Treat!" a chorus of children's voices called from the other side of the door.

Yes, she thought, definitely children who'd gotten a late start.

"Just a moment," she called back. She quickly went to the kitchen for the bowls of candy, came back and, with her arms full, awkwardly unlocked and opened the door.

"Oh my Goodness!"

Standing in front of Belinda was a group of nine children in what had to be the award-winning costume and makeup jobs of the night. The children had apparently sat in makeup chairs for hours in order to turn themselves into the inhabitants of a circus freakshow.

"Trick-or-Treat, Smell-our-Feet, Give us something good to Eat," the children sang and Belinda let out a shocked squeal of joy: no modern -era children ever sang that disgusting little rhyme anymore. The last time she'd heard it was when she'd been a little girl of six and now even five year-old kids simply shouted "Trick-or-Treat" to get on with the business of getting the candy already.

Belinda was simply frozen stiff in her front doorway in amazement, a smile plastered on her face and literally unable to pass out the sweets until she'd taken a good eyeful of the kids in front of her. The young faces and short stature of them all, except for the Giant who seemed to be keeping reasonably good balance on what must have been stilts, were the only things that betrayed that they were actually children in disguise. The children, who had no doubt gone through this same pause at all the houses they'd visited that night, were far from impatient and giggled as they saw that they'd captivated yet another adult.

"Oh, oh, oh, oh, oh my GOODNESS," Belinda repeated, at a loss for anything else to say. "Oh please, you've got to let me take pictures of you; my husband will never believe this. Do you mind waiting for a moment?"

None of the children objected and nodded to each other as if, this too, had been a regular occurrence of their evening. Belinda put the candy bowls down and went sprinting for her camera. She came back quickly and tried to calm herself down so she could take perfect pictures of each one of them.

"What's your name?" she asked the first little girl.

"I'm Harriet the Living Hobbit," she said with a smile. Belinda found her costume perfectly charming: she had on an old-fashioned dress with frills and ruffles and would have passed for a princess had it not been for her huge, bulbous feet, which looked like they had rough, scraggily hair growing out of the toes.

Next was Gorgo the Giant, who's shirt was an animal skin and was still precariously holding on to his balance; every once in a while one of the others would reach out and grab his hip to steady him. Hortense the Bearded Woman was dressed in tights and had a beard glued to her face that was just as rough and scraggily as the hair on Harriet's feet. The poor little thing was scratching at her face and Belinda realized that it was itching her. She guessed that the girl would be ripping it off the second she got back home.

The next two young boys, Mick and Mack as they called themselves, were obviously twin brothers in real life and decided to stitch identical jeans and shirts together in order to become Siamese Twins for the night. The somewhat more disturbing ones were grouped together on her left, including a little girl calling herself "Frederica", who had made up the left half of her face and body to look like that of a boy while the right, down to the small high-heeled shoe on her dainty foot, was quite obviously her real gender. Belinda wondered how much time had gone into her half-man/half-woman clothes.

The two next to her actually made Belinda shudder a bit as she focused on them to take their pictures: Joseph the Elephant Man and Larry the Crab Boy. Joseph's bulbously distorted face must have taken hours to fix up and he wobbled and breathed heavily as if he was having trouble holding it up (possibly the child *was* having trouble maintaining such a heavy prosthetic, she thought). Larry's hands were freaky to say the least: large and pale with the first two fingers missing on each hand, they certainly resembled lobster claws and she was fascinated as she tried to guess how such an effect could look so real right in front of her.

"And what's your name?" she asked the last child.

"I'm the geek," he croaked.

"But what's your name?"

"Just 'the Geek.'"

Son of a method actor, she thought as she lined him up in her viewfinder. His costume was the most real and most disturbing of the bunch, not so much because of the dirty rags and the fake five-o'clock shadow he'd stippled on his face, but because he was carrying in his right hand what looked like an actual, honest-to-God, dead chicken with its head bitten off. Belinda's stomach rolled over slightly to look at it and decided to crop it out of the photo. "So, who are your Mommy and Daddy?"

"They tol' me that m' parents run'd off when I wuz born; they's scared," he said, smiling and showing off his blackened-out teeth. Yes, he'd definitely been poking into one of his parents' acting books and wasn't about to break character. None of the others would give up his name either, which was too bad because she felt that the boy's parents deserved a phone call from her concerning the subject of poor taste. Fun was fun, but there were certain lines that just shouldn't be crossed.

Belinda shook off her discomfort and took in the whole group again, now just a well-disguised group of children again on Halloween. She took fistfuls of candy, more than she had given any of the other children that night, and loaded their waiting bags, which were already close to overflowing.

"I must say that you're all the best bunch of the night," she said. "You all deserve an award for this, or at least your makeup artists do."

Then Gorgo spoke up. "Oh, and don't forget our little friend."

Belinda was amused to hear that, considering everyone standing in front of her, except for Gorgo himself, was little. "And who do you mean by that?"

"Mack, Mick," said Gorgo, "show her."

Despite how charming they all were, Belinda gasped in horror as the twins pulled out a jar with an unborn human fetus floating in it. Belinda knew exactly what it was called, a pickled punk. She had seen a few in her life in films and once up close in an actual sideshow that an old boyfriend had taken her to and they never ceased to horrify her. Although it could have been a clever rubber model taken from some prop-master's shelf, Belinda was almost certain that the punk was real, something that one of their parents had gotten a hold of at some sideshow and loaned out just for this special occasion. This, apparently, was the "trick" part of the visit.

"Kids," she said with a shudder in her voice, "don't you think you're a little too young to be walking around with something like that?"

They looked at each other in confusion. "What do you mean?" asked Harriet. "That's Brian. He's our friend and he wants some candy."

Belinda swallowed and put an extra Milky Way in each of their bags. "Now, it's getting quite late. You don't want your parents to worry, do you? Maybe you should all start to head home."

To her relief, they put Brian back in whatever pocket he'd come from and merrily said "Goodnight" in unison. Belinda closed the door and took a minute to lean against it, catching her breath. The kids must have had other adults object to that horrible thing earlier in their travels and decided not to give any of their real names, since none of them wanted to go home to angry parents. Belinda decided that this was just the sort of thing that would only be a waste of her time and energy to dwell on; after all, what was Halloween night without a good scare?

As soon as she got her mind off little "Brian" in his jar, her smile came back and she laughed with a hand pressed to her mouth so that she might not scream with mirth and scare the neighbors. In all my years, she thought, what a bunch! Oh my Goodness, can you possibly believe…?

She took the nearly empty bowls into the kitchen, and clutched her camera tightly, wanting to do nothing more than upload the photos onto her laptop and email them to Hal. This was just too good to keep to herself.

* * *

When Belinda closed the door on the gang, they stood there, not moving and not speaking until they heard her walk further into the house. At that point, seven of them, groaning as quietly as possible, stood up from the crouch they had been standing in so that the little dummy legs, attached to their clothes, hung limply from their knees. Harriet had been just the right size to pass herself off as a child and Gorgo simply stopped pretending that he was about to fall over and stood up straight.

Their bags were, indeed, practically bursting with sweets and a quick look at Hortense's watch told them that they had just enough time to stroll back down the street to meet the van that would be picking them up to take them back to the circus.

"Thank goodness," Frederica whispered in his low-raspy voice, "that high voice has been killing my throat for the last half hour."

"We're gonna have to thank my Uncle Mel again when we get back," said Larry. "That lady was right: he deserves an award for this."

They murmured and nodded as they started to peel the latex off their faces, which stretched their skin and made the wrinkles disappear even under the most careful scrutiny.

"We get lotso' candy tonight, huh?" asked the Geek. Everyone agreed and tried to keep as far away from him as possible without insulting him; his dead-chicken breath mixed with his almost-total tooth decay was sometimes too much for anyone to take for extended periods.

"Boy," said Mack, falling slightly behind the rest since his brother had sprained his ankle the week before and they were trying to make it down the road on only three good legs, "did you see her eyes when we brought out Brian?" The rest of them giggled.

"I thought her head was gonna explode," gasped Joseph from his heavily deformed mouth.

"Me wanna Brian," demanded the Geek.

"Okay," Mick said, handing him over, "but be careful; don't drop him."

"And don't try to drink him again," said Harriet.

"Me gentle," the Geek said as he held the jar into the moonlight and looked with childish fascination at the little fetus. He laughed creepily to himself.

In the moonlight, the Geek could see that Brian had finally stopped holding his breath and little bubbles were rising to the top of the jar from the hard-to-see gills on either side of his neck.

The Geek never ceased to be amazed by those rising little bubbles. "Brian, we get you candy. You like candy?"

Brian nodded his little head and forced his undeveloped mouth into a smile.

THANKSGIVING

STUFFED

On Wednesday afternoon, Denise Henderson left the supermarket with the last of her Thanksgiving shopping in plastic bags. As she made her way to the car, she looked at her watch and noted the time: 3:25. She shivered, and not just because of the chill in the air or the newly fallen snow that her feet sloshed through. She shivered because of the vial that was tucked safely in her pocketbook. She shivered because, in twenty-four hours, her life was going to be very different than it was right now.

I'm going to do it… I'm really going to do it…

By 3:25 pm on Thanksgiving Day, Denise Henderson knew that the task would be complete: she would officially be a murderer.

Of course, she would be the only one who would know; that was all part of the plan. No slip-ups, no mistakes, no embarrassing questions to answer later on. She'd learned her lines like an actor on opening night on Broadway and often found herself whispering them, under her breath, as she went about her daily tasks…

"Yes, officer, you can see how he was. I was always telling him that he should take better care of himself. He needed to lose weight. The doctor warned him time and time again. But he was stubborn…" The words played on her lips all day long and danced through her head as she typed her letters. She sometimes said them in the mirror, quietly of course, after Harry collapsed into bed for the evening. She'd said them so often she was even beginning to believe them herself. That was a good sign. She knew she was ready.

Denise was nearly at her car when her foot slipped out from under her in the slush. Her arms pinwheeled and grasped the car, just stopping her from falling.

"Oh Denise, are you alright?"

She turned to the voice calling her and saw Karen Schultz walking up to her as fast as she could without falling over. Karen Schultz was in her mid-fifties, a good ten years older than Denise, but her mouth hadn't aged past the age of fifteen considering how incessantly it jabbered when any human ear was within hearing distance.

"Jesus," she said, "you nearly went down! You have to be more careful, you know. You can't just go tearing around the parking lot in weather like this! Although they really should do a better job at clearing out the lot when it snows. I mean, they could get sued if anyone had an accident. You could've broken your leg and taken the whole store away from them! Can you imagine that? I once heard of a woman in Rutland who was lucky enough to step on a banana peel at Shaw's and…"

"I'm fine, Karen," said Denise, finding a moment to speak when the other woman paused for a breath. "Nothing's twisted. Don't worry about a thing."

"Well, give it some time. You never know about these things. You may seem alright now, but I once knew a woman in Nashua who seemed fine after a fall, but when she woke up the next morning…"

"…she was dead, right?"

Karen Schultz was so unprepared for that response that she found herself momentarily silenced and Denise took advantage of the pause to steady herself on her feet and reach for the car door.

"No, of course she wasn't dead! Goodness gracious me, how can you say such a silly thing? No, what I was going to say was..."

Denise was tossing her bags into the passenger seat when she interrupted. "Karen, I hate to rush off, but tomorrow is Thanksgiving and I have a lot to prepare." She got into the front seat and was about to close the door, but found Karen's hand grasping it as she leaned inside.

"Oh, I understand completely. Are you having a lot of people over?"

"Actually, we're having a quiet dinner this year; just me and Harry."

"Oh," Karen said, "that still gives you quite a lot to do anyway..." and she stopped, pursing her lips tightly.

Denise leaned closer to the woman. "What do you mean by that?"

"Nothing, Dear," she answered, "just that there will be lots of food in any case."

Denise felt her face flush and her heart beat quickly. She couldn't believe she was hearing these things. "Karen, if you're making a remark about my husband's..."

But then Denise saw the woman grimace slightly and step back, lightly waving a hand in front of her face. The words fell silent in her mouth.

She can smell it on my breath...

"Oh Denise, I'm sorry if you took offense at anything I said. I always mean the best."

Denise was certain that her face was changing from red to crimson. "That's quite alright. I need to get home now."

"Are you alright to drive? I mean… you nearly had an accident just getting to your car…"

"I slipped! There's snow on the ground."

"Just my point. It's tough enough for *anyone* to get home, let alone someone who… I mean… I just wouldn't be able to live with myself if I allowed a friend of mine to drive home when she's been…"

"Goodbye, Karen!"

Denise yanked the door shut, not caring whether Karen Schultz had time to get her thumb out of the way or not. Karen stumbled backwards slightly as Denise started the car as quickly as she could and put it in gear before it had time to warm up. Before the older woman had time to say anything more, Denise was pulling out of her space and onto the main road.

Karen watched Denise drive away with what she thought was the most sympathetic look a human being could muster. "Poor thing," she said. "Just wait until I tell Ida."

* * *

Denise turned on her favorite Joni Mitchell CD as she drove through the streets towards her home and tried to take her mind off her encounter with Karen Schultz, but the voice in her head kept jabbing at her.

She knew you'd been drinking…

"I only had one scotch," she muttered.

She thought that's why you fell…

"I didn't fall."

She felt so sorry for you. Poor little Denise Henderson, who drinks in the middle of the day and who can't be happy at home, not with that husband of hers. Poor little…

"Shutup!"

Denise pulled into the nearest parking lot she could find and found a spot that she could idle in for a moment. Once the car was parked, she scrunched down in her seat and counted backward from one hundred. By the time she got to forty-six, "Chelsea Morning" was playing on the car speakers and she began to feel the blood draining from her face.

"I will not be embarrassed," she said very carefully. "So what if she knows I had a drink? So what if I've had a drink?"

Denise felt her grip on the wheel relax as she listened to the music and let all thoughts of Karen Schultz leave her mind. The drink she had taken a half hour before had long since lost its potency but that was alright; there was a bottle at home that Harry didn't know about and she would be reaching for it as much as she needed to over the next twenty-four hours. She knew she was embarking on nervy work and would need all the strength she could get.

By the time Joni had gotten to "Woodstock", Denise felt herself breathing deeply and calmly and a smile came to her face. She smiled to think that, by this time tomorrow, the trouble would be over. She would be free of Harry. She would never be embarrassed again.

Denise put the car in reverse, pulled out of the space and headed for home.

* * *

It was one o'clock in the afternoon the following day when the extra-large bird came out of the oven, golden-brown and ready to be carved. She'd been preparing far into the evening the night before and cooking all morning and the house smelled of succulent gluttony. She imagined that Harry was tortured by the aroma as he sat on the couch in the living room, watching *Chitty Chitty Bang Bang* on television. He would be sniffing up every sniff in the apartment since he wouldn't have the strength to actually get up to make a nuisance of himself in the kitchen. Once upon a time, she would have to shoo him out every fifteen minutes or so; now he simply called from the living room "Is it ready yet" and "How much longer" from time to time. And Denise worked harder than she'd ever worked before to produce the perfect Thanksgiving dinner for her husband; after all, if this meal was destined to be his last, the least she could do was make it the most memorable of his life.

"Will it be much longer?" Harry shouted from the living room as soon as Dick Van Dyke had finished singing "The Old Bamboo".

"Just give it some time, honey," she called back, finishing the carving and finding herself with a plate of expertly sliced meat that starving children could have lived on for a month. "I'll tell you when!"

Harry thankfully went back to his movie and Denise was left preparing the rest of the trimmings: the giblet gravy came out perfectly for what was probably the first time in her life, the maple syrup melted exquisitely into the carrots, and the potatoes were whipped into a light, fluffy mash. Denise fought a childish urge to break out the digital camera and snap the entire spread for one of those magazines that housewives were supposed to fawn over. It looked beautiful just sitting in bowls and serving dishes; once she had it on the plates and on the table, it would be a masterpiece.

Of course, she wondered if any magazine would print such a photo if they discovered that a man had died after eating it. Probably not.

Denise turned her attention to the stuffing, sitting in a blue bowl on the counter. It looked delicious, and she had followed her mother's recipe to the comma. And now it was time to deviate from it. Denise opened up one of the nearby junk drawers that Harry never fiddled through and took out the vial that she had secreted there the day before. The liquid inside was light brown in color and would blend well with the stuffing. The woman at the dark shop, who had led her down the creaky stairs into the basement when Denise had produced a wad of bills that proved she was serious in what she required, had assured her that the light brown liquid was just the thing that she was looking for. For the type of money that Denise had paid, saved over the period of a full year, she had been guaranteed something without taste or odor, something that could hide in food and innocently slip down Harry's throat where it could do its good work. And once done, it would hide from the all-seeing eyes of the professional who would search later for a reason as to why Harry Henderson had fallen asleep on the couch after Thanksgiving dinner and never woken up again. Of course, Denise didn't think there would be any question whatsoever. It would be obvious to anyone with one working eye and half a brain. And if it wasn't, that's when her well-rehearsed lines would make their debut.

"I told him to go easy," she murmured as she poured the contents of the bottle into the stuffing and began mixing it in. "The doctor told him he would end up like this one day."

The small bottle was nearly empty when Denise suddenly held back the last few drops and gasped. She was so caught up in what she knew would be the aftermath of the meal that she'd forgotten something that the woman had said to her.

"Not too much, my dear. Very powerful stuff, this is. You'll not need more than a quarter of the vial to do the job for you."

Denise looked at the bowl of stuffing in front of her, now sopping with the new ingredient. The vial in her hand was nearly empty.

"Denise," Harry called out from the living room, "is it ready yet?"

"Just about," she called back. "Nearly there!"

He's a big guy… he probably needs extra to do the job properly… no turning back now anyway…

Denise finished mixing the stuffing, scooped it and the plate of sliced turkey up and crossed to the kitchen table. As she placed the serving plates, she called out, "It's on the table: come and get it!" Even though she had only two of the nine serving plates on the table, she knew she'd have enough time to set the rest before Harry got off the couch and walked the twelve steps to his chair.

The food was on the table and Denise was emerging from the kitchen with an opened bottle of white wine when Harry finally made his appearance. Although Harry's doctor continually warned him that his weight had gone far past all semblance of control and that it would kill him soon if he didn't do something about it, the doctor secretly wondered what it was that was keeping the forty-six year-old tollbooth operator going. At three hundred and forty-six pounds, Harry could move no faster than a slow waddle as he made his way to the kitchen table, his breath chugging and slurping with every waddling step. He put a hand on the wall to steady himself and Denise secretly pitied the wall. But she almost immediately envied the wall since it had no nose with which to inhale the musk that was Harry's constant companion. A mixture of sweat and gas from both ends threatened to swallow the pleasant aroma of the dinner that she'd spent all morning preparing. He lurched painfully from the wall to the back of his chair and pulled himself the rest of the way. He pulled the chair out the necessary distance from the table, it seemed like a mile away to Denise, and collapsed so heavily into it that Denise was glad that they lived on the first floor. Once sat, he let out a huge, sighing breath that nearly curled the hairs in Denise's nose.

Look at it this way... he's going the way he would want to... he couldn't possibly last much longer anyway... I'm just giving him a nudge... helping him along...

Denise started piling turkey, potatoes, corn, yams, carrots, cranberry sauce and, of course, stuffing onto Harry's plate, which was his special, extra-large plate. His eyes glistened in his head as he watched the food landing in front of him, never looking up at the long-suffering woman who had provided it for him. In a final act, she placed the entire plate of biscuits within groping distance and flanked his plate with a tub of butter on one side and the gravy boat on the other. The contented, snorkeling purr that rose from Harry's throat was the sound of a man who was about to enter the closest thing to sheer bliss that his waking life could dish up.

Denise crossed to the opposite side of the table and sat down, her plate still empty. Just as she sat, Harry crossed himself and said a breathy groaning prayer.

"God is Grace. God is Good. Let us thank you for our food. Amen." He dug in before the final word was completely out of his mouth. Denise reached for the assorted plates and started serving herself.

Only once during the dinner did Harry look up at his wife and speak.

"You're not having any stuffing?"

"Watching my weight," she replied, sampling as much of the turkey as her churning stomach could muster.

* * *

Harry had never been an athlete, had never had anything approaching an athlete's body even when he was young, and Denise supposed that she had loved him in their early days and even thought his plumpness had been kind of cute. But that was seventeen years before and Harry's diet had deteriorated to the point that he resembled a shambling creature rather than the man she'd married. His insistence on putting more and more food into his face had meant nothing but loss for Denise: loss of attraction and sexual fulfillment, loss of funds as the grocery bill got bigger and bigger, and especially loss of her own self-esteem as she found herself lawfully bound to a man who demanded the unwanted attention of anyone who glanced in his direction. How people stared; how they looked in horror at the sight of the human frame blown out beyond all proportions of health and decency. She couldn't blame them: Harry's body invited rapt attention. It wasn't humanly possible to discretely ignore him as he waddled down the street. They caught sight of him, they stared, and most horribly, their faces expressed shock, horror and disgust. She could almost hear the thoughts of the enraptured gazes as they stared despite whatever their parents had taught them:

"How can anyone get that big?"

"Couldn't anyone stop him?"

"Does he know he's that big?"

"How does that poor woman stand him?"

"How did those two end up together?"

"That poor woman…"

That poor woman… that poor woman… that poor woman…

The day was November the 26th and Denise was certain that it was the last day of embarrassment of her life, the last day that she would ever be referred to, even in silent thought, as "that poor woman". Instead, she imagined how the new conversations about her would go as she scraped the gravy from Harry's plate in the sink.

She looks a new woman since the funeral… she'll be alright… she's still good-looking at her age… soon a nice man will come along and…

Denise held the bowl that held the stuffing over the sink and rinsed it thoroughly with detergent. The last remnants would be gone as soon as she put it into the dishwasher. She was almost sorry to see it washed away, the handy, tidy little brew that would do what mountains of food had, for some reason, failed to do all these years.

"Expansion," the woman in the shop had said.

"I don't I quite follow you," she'd replied.

"Just a little bit of this mixture, evenly distributed in his food, will expand his heart to the point of bursting. From what you've told me, his heart will be enlarged to capacity, correct?"

Yes, this was the way. His heart was probably the size of an elephant's ballsack by now. Something was holding it back from total meltdown, from the blood breaking through the muscle wall and completing what he'd started years ago with his second and third helpings at every meal. She was just nudging it slightly. She...

"Denise!"

He was calling from the living room. After dinner, he'd lumbered to get out of his chair and back to the couch in time to watch the first of several hundred showings over the course of the next month of "It's A Wonderful Life". The last thing he'd said as he finally gave up the battle against the multitude in front of him was "I'm stuffed." She'd thought it was the last thing he'd ever say to her.

"Denise, I don't feel so good!"

"Don't you?" she said quietly to herself. Her heart started beating fast as she realized that this was it: this was the moment that she'd thought about for so long.

"Denise, I... I think I'm gonna...

I won't go in there, she thought. Best not to. Whatever he does, it will be the last abomination. I'll sell the couch and all the furniture once he's gone. Sell it? Hell, I'll just build a bonfire. Who'd want to buy it anyway, with the smells and the broken springs and worn foam? He'll make a mess – that's what Harry does best – but I'll let it be just this one last time… I'll just put up with it this one last…

And then Harry's voice called again, like water struggling to run through a clogged drain.

"Denise! I'm… I'm…"

And then there was a sound like the seat of a wicker chair letting go under tremendous weight: a squeaky creak that raised the hair on Denise's head. She couldn't stop herself from calling him.

"Harry?"

And then she heard a loud, wet blast followed by a splash and a groan that could only be Harry's dying breath. Denise dropped a plate into the sink as she replayed the sounds in her mind. The old woman had said nothing about a loud blast, so loud that it must've carried into the hallway. In fact, she said that Harry's heart would burst quietly in his ribcage and there would only be a…

She heard a high-pitched, incessant, mechanical whine. Harry had somehow managed to set off the smoke alarm.

Her jaw trembled as she backed away from the sink, realizing that something had gone terribly wrong. Her feelings were confirmed when she heard someone, most likely Mrs. Roth from across the hall, banging on the front door.

"Excuse me," the woman's voice called between poundings, "is everything alright in there? I heard a funny noise!"

Denise ran into the living room where she'd expected to find Harry quietly expired and the smell brought her to a halt a few feet from the couch. There was no need to go further: in the dim light from the television, she could see everything.

Harry's chest and stomach had exploded: blood, offal and bits that could only be chunks of chewed, undigested food lay in an ever expanding radius in front of his body. The coffee table, carpet, television and stereo were dripping in murk that had been trapped inside him only a moment before. Incredibly, smoke was rising from his decimated stomach and shattered ribcage and had drifted into the grill of the smoke detector. The entire room was covered in a sick, gaseous smell that hung like a wet, thick fog. Denise felt her dinner rise in her throat and forced herself to keep it down.

And the banging on the door continued.

"Mrs. Henderson, are you alright in there?"

"Is something wrong?" The voice of the landlord, approaching.

"There was this weird sound – like an explosion – and I can hear the smoke alarm going off. I think something must've happened to their stove!"

"Aw Jesus, what the Hell is that smell?"

"It's awful!"

"Just wait here while I go get the key."

Denise stood in her spot, shaking but unable to move otherwise. The blood, slowly gurgling into the carpet and settling in thick pools, held her attention. She repeated the lines she'd learned under her breath and realized they sounded idiotic under the new circumstances.

Before she realized that any time had passed, she heard a click in the door: the landlord was inserting his passkey.

Oh my God, they're coming in! I can't stop them! They'll come in and see this mess! There's no way I can explain away any of this. They mustn't come in! They mustn't see…

The top bolt clicked back and Denise could hear the landlord fumbling for the doorknob key. She took two steps and stood in front of her dead, decimated husband, her blood boiling in her brain.

"Honestly," she shouted, "sometimes I think you *live* to embarrass me!"

CHRISTMAS

CHRISTMAS LIGHTS

Jack O'Sullivan wrapped himself in his warmest coat, a colorful scarf and put on his warm boots before crashing back onto the couch for ten minutes and pondering what the Hell the point was of going out, besides the fact that he was already dressed for it. His therapist had said that he needed to get out more often, and suggested that he force himself out of the apartment at least once a day even if he had nowhere to go, which was the case most of the time. Since he'd lost his job, Jack didn't like leaving the apartment during the daytime, afraid that the phone would ring just at the moment when he walked beyond earshot with news that a new job was his for the asking. He didn't much like sitting at his desk at home day after day, blinded by the sunlight that always hit him through the blinds that refused to close properly, and going through the online job markets but he didn't see any other solution to his problem. No matter how fired up he got himself at eight o'clock in the morning when he'd switch the computer on, by ten o'clock he would be thoroughly depressed and his output would trickle to one resume emailed every hour (if that). The phone only rang when some dialing machine decided it was time to bug him about a new credit card offer. The days went on and on, blending into one another until he began to not notice when the weekend rolled around. Indeed, though the calendar told him it was December 8th, practically any thoughts that Christmas was approaching were almost completely driven from his mind.

No money, no job, no decent food in the house and no real plans for Christmas, he thought as he sat on the couch, sweating in his warm coat. This was not the way he'd seen life progressing as he headed headlong into his forties. No, the major book deal that he was expecting had apparently gotten lost in the mail. His typing fingers had slowed down in the last few weeks as he thought about the bills that wouldn't be paid and the late fees and phone calls that were surely just over the horizon.

But it was after five o'clock. The sun had just set and Jack looked out his second floor window between the buildings across the street and into the neighborhood of residential houses that lay just beyond. Colored twinkles were already cutting through the gray dusk: Christmas lights were being switched on down there.

Jack's own neighborhood was mostly apartment complexes, so tenants hung their holiday lights only on the railings of their terraces and very few of his neighbors made the effort to show off any holiday spirit. Jack grumbled to himself about how he'd avoided putting up his own lights so far this year, a task that usually occupied the bulk of the day following Thanksgiving. He looked around his dark apartment and knew that he certainly wouldn't find any inspiration within its walls. Now that it was past five and no one with a job was going to call at this point, he thought it might be a good idea to go out and try to find out how people who were already feeling the spirit of the season were expressing themselves.

"Looking at houses I don't live in, housing people I don't know who'll have a much happier Christmas than I will. Can't say that this will make me feel better."

But it would, and he knew it. He could breathe the cold air that always invigorated him and, with each brightly lit house, remember how the lights on his parents' house had delighted him as a child. Even inside his depressed and unfocused mind, the lights stirred an old, sizzling kernel of feeling, begging to pop.

Go, go, go, what else can you do?

Jack half-smiled and stood up. In less than ten seconds, the keys were in his pocket and he was out the door.

It wasn't a long walk, six or seven minutes at most to walk out of his own quiet neighborhood, lit only by old and tired streetlamps, and to cross Magnolia Boulevard, which wasn't easy with the sun set and rush hour still in progress. But Jack finally made it across the street and walked into the residential neighborhood where, only two houses in, he was greeted by a good and tasteful light display. The outlines of the walls and roof were lined with blue and white lights. Electric candles with yellow bulbs were set in the windows and low lights within the house made the Christmas tree perfectly visible to him in the street. Two shrubs that stood on either side of the front path displayed strings of red lights in a spiral pattern from their bases to their crowns. Jack patted his coat and cursed himself for not bringing his MP3 player so that he could listen to carols during his excursion and then decided that it was better to listen only to the cold air as it whipped around him. He thought that maybe he would get lucky and hear the snatches of tunes coming from some of the houses and that it really wasn't a good idea to go walking around in the dark with his ears plugged, no matter how ordinary the neighborhood was. He took a moment to take in the display at the first house and then continued into the neighborhood.

At the first intersection, Tyler and Jones, Jack could just barely see a sign on a telephone pole that he knew warned suspicious travelers of the local neighborhood watch program and that his progress would be noted if he tried any funny business. He'd seen the sign many times during his previous walks in the daylight and mused that he was, while in the neighborhood, not so much in danger of being jumped by a gang but by concerned parents mistaking him for a thug. He looked left and right and was briefly puzzled: though the sun had set, there were no lights on display on any of the houses to his right and the road straight ahead was equally dark. To the left, he could see white lights on one house about thirty or forty yards down; the rest were just as dark as the other alternative paths.

The decision was easy to make, but Jack still stood at the intersection, looking in all directions. "Where the Hell are all the lights?" he muttered to himself. "Is it too early in the month?" Deciding that it had to get better further into the neighborhood, he turned left and walked towards the lone, lighted house.

Neither tasteful nor gaudy, Jack slowly came to a stop as he got to the house. A few strings were attached helter skelter to the house in a manner that could only be described as half-assed. The large front yard and iron fence that guarded the house remained dark. Equally dark were the windows. There was no sign that anyone was home: no parked car in the driveway and no sounds or movement whatsoever from the house. Jack realized that the lights had been left on a timer that had activated and wondered why no timer had activated the lights inside. He couldn't tell if there was a Christmas tree inside and the whole scene depressed him. It was as if an initial burst of spirit had been squelched and abandoned.

Abandoned… now there's a funny word…

Jack put his gloved hands on the fence and tried to look deeper into the dark windows. The house didn't feel like it was waiting for its inhabitants to come home after a hard day at the office. It felt abandoned.

He looked at the darkened houses surrounding him. He couldn't see any cars in any driveways or parked along the sidewalk. The windows were all dark; not shuttered, just dark.

For the first time, Jack realized that there was no one else walking on the street.

Where is everybody?

Absently, he started walking past the partially-lit house, paying attention only to the puzzle that was spinning around his mind so quickly that it wouldn't let him solve it.

Where is everyone? I mean… yes, I know it's not that long after five and people are probably still on their way home from work. That makes sense. And it is still a bit early in the month, so there's no problem with the bulk of the houses not having their lights up yet. This weekend, for sure. Just wait and you'll see by Sunday this whole section

*will be lit up like one gigantic Christmas tree and parents will be taking
their kids all over to see each others' houses and…*

And Jack stopped walking.

*Where are the kids? Sure, most of the adults will be on their way
back from work, but the kids would've been home from school hours ago.
Even if they're not going outside because of the cold, they'd have the
lights on. Some would be out walking their dogs. I can't hear any
barking. I can't hear anything except the wind and me. There's nobody
here! Maybe I should…*

Jack snapped fully awake and looked around, squinting in the
dark. The street he was on had no lit houses at all. The last house with
Christmas lights that he had seen was nowhere in sight. He tried to see if
there was a street sign in the vicinity, but it was too dark to see.

"Where am I?"

*Don't be silly. This is a neighborhood that you've walked
through dozens of times. You can't possibly be…*

Lost.

Jack's hands began to shiver inside his gloves. So lost had he
been in thought that he couldn't remember which direction he'd been
standing in when he came to himself again. And as he noted before, the
streets were deserted and not a single light, Christmas or otherwise,
shone from the foreboding houses around him.

"Hello," he said, not loudly because of an odd reluctance, an old
habit that forced him to speak softly in the darkness so as not to wake
anyone up.

There's no one to wake up.

"Hello!"

He said it much louder that time, almost shouting. No one answered.

"HELLO!"

The word rang and echoed.

Jack started walking quickly in the direction he was facing in, not sure if he was heading back the way he came or not. After fifteen or twenty steps, he found himself at an intersection that opened only to the right. Looking down the street, he was relieved to see at least three homes decorated tastefully in Christmas lights and a few cars parked along the side of the road, although there was still no one walking in the street. Still, it was a great deal more welcoming than the streets he had already passed through so he turned right and headed for the lights.

Jack was a bit surprised to see that the first parked car he came to turned out to be a police car. As far as he could see, there was no one inside and it was as dark and silent as the house it sat in front of. "It must be the cop's house," he murmured. "He drove the squad car home and…"

But again, the house was dark. No life, no warmth, no nothing.

Jack was walking past the squad car when he noticed a change in the texture of the ground beneath his boots, different from the rocks, pebbles and leaves he'd been stepping on from time to time.

Broken glass…

Jack squinted in the darkness at the squad car and saw that the driver's window was shattered. Peering further, he could see the same had happened to the opposite window. Looking around guiltily, Jack tried the door and found it unlocked. He opened it and leaned in; no lights came on and he had to squint. As he expected, broken glass covered the two seats and, in what little moonlight there was, he almost imagined that the subtle changes in color and texture on the seats just might be because of dried splatters of blood.

Okay... scared now...

Jack tried to feel towards the dashboard, mindful of the broken glass, in hopes of finding the police radio but drew his hand back when it met with only a mangled collection of metal and dead wires.

He jumped back from the car, leaving the door open, and turned towards the lit houses, the closest of which was still a full block away. Despite the freezing air making it harder and harder to move, Jack hurried as fast as he could towards the house.

But then there was the sound of a crash... of wood splintering and bursting apart.

And then a woman screaming.

"No! No, don't you dare! My baby... NO!"

And then a scream that was not words just before all the lights on the house went dark.

Jack stopped, cold and confused, and only dimly thought about how he was in the middle of the street... how he could be seen if...

If what? What's happening over there?

And then from in the house, still a block away, there was a sound that made Jack fall to one knee in the middle of the street.

Was that a growl?

He could hear furniture being overturned and the crash of dishes as they fell to the floor. Something was happening and Jack wanted to see what it was. He was rooted to the spot, stuck on one knee, until he realized that the sounds of destruction had stopped.

GET OUT OF THE STREET!

Too cold to make a decent job of it, Jack lunged stiffly across the street, straining his knee and forcing him to roll into the opposite curb. He had barely come to rest when he raised his head and saw it emerge from the darkened house.

Lit dimly from the houses further up the road, Jack saw only its silhouette as it ran on two bent, skinny legs and stopped suddenly in the middle of the street. Its legs were long, but bent in a crouch, as if it were ready to spring. Its arms remained fixed in front of it, reaching with pointed fingers or claws extended. It turned its pointed head around and snarled, looking and perhaps smelling for anything that may have had the misfortune to cross into its path. A long, beak-like mouth pointed skywards and it howled, locking all of Jack's limbs into a tight wad of fear.

After one more look around, it darted for a tree and simply ran straight up its length until it reached the fragile branches at the top. Just as one branch snapped under its weight, it leaped and landed cleanly on the roof of the closest house and ran across it without pausing. It leaped again onto a neighboring roof, changed direction and was gone.

Jack remained motionless, lying in the hollow of the curb, hearing the leaves and branches dislodged from the creature's ascent still falling to the ground even though it was long gone.

Is it long gone?

Fifteen minutes passed while he lay in the street, his ears fine-tuned to the sound of the night. He heard the ambiance of the street and the rip of the wind and listened for any sound of movement. He heard none. With an effort he'd never known before, Jack coaxed his body to push itself off the cold concrete, fought an urge to continue on all fours and lifted himself up, slightly crouched and stifling a groan as his stiff back barked at him. He started walking, very slowly, up the street towards the house that the creature had sprung from. The houses further on that had their lights on before the attack were still lit. As Jack moved closer to the scene of the attack, he squinted and thought he saw someone peeping through the window of one of the further lit houses. He nearly broke into a run when a window curtain, hastily drawn, obscured the watcher and the house's lights switched off a moment later. There were no screams like the last time: the inhabitants simply wanted no part of whoever it was that they'd seen wandering the streets; he was no concern of those who were locked up safely behind their doors.

But they're not safe...

Jack slowly made his way to the open gate of the house that the creature had emerged from. Even in the dark, it was easy to see that the door had been smashed in. A nearby window had been smashed out and, amazingly enough, a toilet lay on the wet grass. It would've been funny if it wasn't for...

...everything, he thought. Everything is wrong.

The other house, even further up, that still had its lights on followed suit with its neighbor and went dark, but Jack barely noticed. He staggered up the path and entered through the remains of the shattered door.

He immediately kicked and stepped on broken glass and porcelain that was strewn all over the floor. It was hard to see in the darkened house and Jack was not about to switch a light on. The moonlight creeping in through the windows allowed him to make out the picture frames smashed on the floor of the foyer. A few steps in and he could see the entrance to the living room to his right. The Christmas tree was lying on its side in a bed of broken ornaments and lights. It looked more than just pushed over; Jack imagined that it had been jumped on over and over again, in an effort to squash the life out of it.

Jack took his eyes away from it and looked ahead to see the stairs leading up. The banister had been torn out of its foundation and strewn on the floor below. The wall on the side of the stairs was clawed all the way up; huge chunks of wallpaper and plaster littered the steps.

I'm not going up there, Jack thought and started climbing.

He nearly fell in the dark twice, what with all the debris beneath his feet, but he made it up to the second floor landing. That is, he made it far enough up the stairs to see what was laying on the landing.

The woman's body had been literally gutted, ripped down the center and opened wide. The moonlight through the upper windows shined on the gouts of blood that swamped the walls and carpet. The body was nearly empty beneath her ribs: her stomach, lungs, liver and heart had been taken away.

*No, it was empty-handed when I saw it. It ate her... right here...
it ate her...*

And then Jack looked beyond her body into the bedroom and saw
what it had done to her baby.

He stepped back, knowing it could be suicide but unable to help
himself. He stepped on a chunk of plaster and stumbled backwards. His
arms flailed and reached out for the banister that wasn't there. He fell
and half of his body hit the stairs while his legs flailed in midair. He felt
himself bouncing towards the drop and he reared his legs up. The
momentum kept him from going over the drop but also pushed him
rolling and tumbling down the rest of the stairs. He howled in pain as
every nerve in his body struck an edge on his way down. The last thing
he remembered was seeing the front doorway rear up towards him
upside-down.

* * *

The upside-down doorway was also his first sight upon wakening.
He stared at it, trying to remember what party he was at and how much
he'd drunk before he'd passed out. Then he saw the shards of wood and
slivers of glass littering the floor.

Remembering, he strained to spring up, but immediately fell on
his side again as his bruises and joints, stiffened from the cold, screamed.
He bit back a yell. Slowly, with meticulous care, Jack picked himself off
the floor, wincing at each move. When he was finally on his feet, he
took two steps and felt a screech rise to his throat. Both his knees and his
lower back ached, although he was sure nothing was broken. When all

the pains momentarily subsided, he took a deep breath and looked at his watch.

It had smashed on his way down the stairs. The fall had taken place at 6:36.

The direction of the moon shadows outside told him that it was a lot later than 6:36. Jack hugged himself against the cold and slowly limped out the front door. From what he could see, not a single light burned in any house in the vicinity, Christmas or otherwise. The moon provided his only light, and that didn't allow him to see more than a few feet ahead of him.

If anything comes at me… if that THING comes at me… I won't know until it's too late… Maybe I should stay here until morning… maybe it won't come back here… maybe…

But Jack thought of the woman's carcass upstairs, consumed and thrown aside like an old banana peel, and limped into the street. He picked a direction at random and started walking.

It seemed like hours passed as he stumbled slowly through the neighborhood streets, seeing no house nor landmark that he recognized, and choosing his directions blindly. At one point, he realized that he was murmuring "Help" with every pained step that he took, and forced himself to keep quiet for fear that he might attract attention.

Just as he reached a left turn and was close enough to the sign at its corner to read the words "Not A Thru Way", Jack heard something behind him: far off and high above, the creak of wood and shingles as something leaped and landed. He whimpered and leaned forward to hold the signpost tight for fear that he might pass out from fright.

Keep still… keep quiet…

He shut his eyes when he realized the thing was somewhere behind him. For the sake of curiosity, to look and see what it was that was going to kill him, Jack opened them again and was about to turn around when he looked down the dead end street and saw something that made his heart leap.

Christmas lights!

On a house about forty yards away, Christmas lights were still burning. Despite everything from the chest down aching, Jack broke into a lumbering run. He audibly panted and moaned as he made his way up the street and hoped he could drown out the snarl coming from behind him. He felt dizzy, but he shook his head clear and ran on. As the house got closer and closer, the lights became more and more brilliant. He'd never seen a house so bright and dazzling. He coughed and spit up bile into the street, running harder and faster.

The growl coming from the street sign, where he had been standing only a few minutes before, pushed him the rest of the way until he was charging through the gate and up the walkway.

He dimly registered that the lights were blinding, that there must have been thousands of bulbs, all different colors, burning from the roof, windows, walls, trees, shrubs and fences. His amazement at the sheer grandiose sight didn't stop him from lunging to the door and pounding on it.

"Help me!" he screamed. "Something's coming! It's right behind me! Please, let me in!"

The sound of leaves and debris behind kicked aside by running feet... that horrible snarl...

"PLEASE OPEN THE..."

The door flew open and a hand grabbed his jacket and pulled his already falling body inside. He tried to twist around to see what was behind him, but the door slammed shut and, as he hit the floor, two hands pressed tightly against it and waited for the impact.

It hit the door with a massive bang, but the door held. The thing outside roared in frustration and Jack could hear his rescuer murmuring something, a chant repeated over and over again. The two of them remained where they were for a few minutes, both of them too afraid to move. Finally, the person put an ear to the door. After a moment, she turned to Jack.

"Wow," she said. "I won't ask what happened to you; I can guess."

She looked to be in her fifties, starting to gray but still smooth in the face. She wore jeans that covered her round hips and Jack guessed that her loose sweater covered a slightly bulging belly. Her bare feet were pale in the dark carpet. She slowly moved towards him and knelt down.

"My name's Marion Klum. I'll help you to the table."

* * *

2:30.

According to Marion Klum's Mickey Mouse wall clock, it was 2:30 in the morning. Jack couldn't take his eyes off the clock as Marion bustled behind him at the stove.

I left the house at five, he thought. I must've been unconscious for hours... or wandering for hours. And it never came back to get me... it never... until... it...

"It," he said, quietly. He whipped around to see Marion Klum still fussing at the stove. "What is it?"

"Let me just get you this cup of..."

"Tell me: what is it?" His voice rose as he tried to rise out of his chair, despite the aches. Marion turned to him, a dripping, chocolate-covered spoon in her hand.

"You're in my house, now. So you'll behave."

Or she'll kick me out, he thought. Would she really do that?

Jack decided that this wasn't the moment to test the woman who had saved him. He edged back into his chair with tiny grunts. A moment later, she placed a mug filled with hot cocoa in front of him and sat down opposite him. She simply looked at him silently as he placed his thawing hands on the mug and took a good, long drink. The cocoa burned as it went down, but he didn't care: it was good to get a strong jolt of warmth in him after lying out in the cold for hours.

"I'll tell you what I know," she said, "and you'll just have to accept the fact that I don't know everything."

"What is it?" he asked again.

She sighed. "Looks like I'm gonna disappoint you right away."

He waved the answer away. "Alright, can you tell me how long this has been going on?"

"A couple of weeks now. It started a few days after

Thanksgiving. I remember the first night it happened; just up the street a bit, around 10:30 at night, that's when I heard the scream and the crash." She stopped as she looked towards the closest window, remembering when she stood and watched as it happened the first time. "A friend of mine, Gladys Tinsbury, was the first one it got. After the scream, I ran to the window and saw her front door explode out like someone fired a cannon behind it. That thing just... leaped into the middle of the street. It just ran for the nearest tree and..."

"It ran straight up it," Jack finished for her. "I saw it do it myself. It's the damnedest thing to see."

"Yeah. If you saw it on television, you'd laugh. But on your own street in the middle of the night..."

"Stop," he said, holding a hand up, "you don't have to tell me. So this thing killed your friend?"

Marion fell silent for a moment before nodding. "Others ran over to see what happened, but I couldn't go because I saw it. They didn't, but I did. I just couldn't go over and see her." A tear fell out of her eye, but only one tear before she got hold of herself again.

"What happened when the police arrived?"

"Well..." she began, but Jack suddenly cut her off as his memory kicked in.

"Oh, wait a minute. I saw a police car on the street. The windows and radio were busted and..." The full force of what was happening in the neighborhood finally dawned on him. "There was dried blood on the seats."

"That's not the only empty police car out there," she said. "Over the next few days, more police showed up. None of them made it this far."

"It attacks during the day too?"

"No, it sleeps during the day."

"Then why haven't you gotten out? Why can't the police come in during the day?"

Marion looked at the table, debating on whether she should tell him what she knew he wouldn't believe. "We sleep during the day, too."

"What?"

"It makes us go to sleep... somehow, it..."

Jack got out of his chair and started to pace around the table, never taking his eyes off Marion Klum. "What, cast spells? You're saying this neighborhood is haunted by some creature that can tear people apart, skip over trees and houses *and* cast spells to make everyone fall asleep so they can't escape? You expect me to believe that?"

Marion didn't look up at him. In a tired voice, she said, "You're right. I'm putting you on. You can go now." She rose and started for the door.

Jack felt his heart beginning to race. "If all that was going on, they'd find a way to deal with it..."

"Yes, you're probably right."

"They'd surround the neighborhood with cops... the National Guard even... it would be all over the news..."

"No doubt." She was at the door and starting to draw back the bolt.

"For Christ's sake, the friends and family of everyone on these streets would be out there! There'd be panic! There's no way that this could be kept quiet."

"You've seen right through me," she said, turning the doorknob.

"Stop!" he shouted. The door was opened a crack and Marion simply stood there, waiting. Jack fell back into his chair. "I'll listen, I promise. Just... don't make me go back out there."

Marion closed and locked the door and came back to the kitchen. She sat down opposite Jack and looked at him squarely.

"Now, listen: I don't know and can't speak for what's going on out beyond the neighborhood. It's like a different world, now; one that only exists when I'm lucky enough to dream about it. Maybe the police have given up after losing so many men. Maybe there's been high level meetings in the state capitol about us, and they decided what they didn't know wouldn't hurt them. As for family and friends..." she trailed off briefly as she stole a glance at the phone on the wall. "Back before that thing out there cut all the phone lines, I called my son in Glendale and told him... made him swear on a stack of Bibles... to stay away from here. I can only imagine other families did the same thing. All I know is that we're alone here, cut off, and that's the way it's gonna stay unless I can find a way to..."

Marion bit her bottom lip as if she'd caught herself saying too much. Jack looked closely at her. "What do you think you can do?" he asked.

"I'm not sure. There are some books..."

"Does this have anything to do with what you were muttering when I first came in?" he asked. Marion scrunched up her face and Jack thought he detected shame. "You had something to do with this, didn't you?"

"No!" she said sharply. "It was Gladys!"

"The one who got killed on the first night," he said. "How did it start?"

Marion choked back a throb in her throat and spoke softly. "We'd both studied the occult throughout most of our lives..."

"Witchcraft?"

Marion was quick to correct him. "I've never done anything that could've caused that thing. But, in the weeks leading up to it, Gladys kept talking about something she'd found... a new book..."

"What, like something out of Lovecraft?"

"Just because a writer made up stories about cursed books and demons doesn't mean that they don't actually exist, right?"

Jack leaned forward, wanting to say something to dash her entire theory as a lonely and frightened woman's crazed imagination, but he was too enraptured. "You think she found some book somewhere and said the wrong words..."

"I said before that I couldn't go over to look at her when that thing got her, but the neighbors told me that when they found her, lying in a pool of blood were the ripped pages of a book. I think she lost control of whatever she called into being and..."

"…and then it destroyed the instructions on how to send it away." Jack couldn't believe that he'd said it with the steady, solid conviction of a man giving the weather report. Marion turned and indicated the bookshelf against the far wall in the living room.

"I have my own books, but nothing like what she must've got her hands on to create that thing. When I tell you that I don't know what it is, that's the truth; there's nothing like it in anything I've ever read." Marion slumped back in her chair, tired and embarrassed to have confessed so much to a total stranger.

"You know enough to keep yourself protected, though," he said. "That's what you were chanting when I came in; some sort of protection charm?"

Marion nodded and started to rise. "If I do it right, it should be strong enough for both of us. Come on."

Jack's back stiffened. "Come on?"

"I'm gonna take you back."

"Out there?" Jack asked. Now his jaw got stiff as well.

"Well, since Santa Claus isn't coming to fly you back, there isn't really any other way, is there?"

"But…"

"The sun will be up in three hours and then you and I will fall down wherever we are and lay there until 5:08 tomorrow night… excuse me… tonight. Trust me; you don't want to stay here more than one night."

Marion was putting on her coat and boots and Jack was shocked to realize that in less than a minute's time, he would be back out there on the street where that thing was.

"I'll do my best to protect us both," she said, "Now we really have to..."

Jack decided he wasn't ready and found another question to ask. "But if you can move protected through the neighborhood, why haven't you led your neighbors out by now?"

Marion sighed. "They're afraid of me. They know that Gladys had something to do with that thing running loose and they know I was her friend. Now if there's nothing else..."

"But wait," Jack said as Marion rolled her eyes, "the lights. I would think that it would attack houses with lights on. But some people still have lights on and your house is visible from blocks away. What's that about?"

Marion walked back to him and looked down at him. Jack felt himself lost in her sad eyes, as if she was trying to draw the fear out of him. "At first, people turned their lights off because they thought they'd be safe. Then it started attacking dark houses. Some lights went back on and some stayed off. It went for bright houses some nights and dark houses other nights. Eventually everyone was confused as to what they could do to be safe. But I can see now that it was just enjoying the hunt." She gently took his hand and started rubbing it. "It's playing with us. It has a killing field full of cattle and it wants to enjoy itself as much as it can."

Suddenly, there was a loud thump on the roof and they both looked up. They heard a second thump further down the length of the house and then the rustling of the branches of the tree next door. Marion looked back down at Jack.

"I keep my lights on so that anyone caught wandering the streets at night might find me. I figure it is the least I can do. Now, if there's nothing else…"

There was nothing else.

* * *

The cold was even more bitter as they walked through the streets of the neighborhood now that Jack knew that there was nothing he could do to protect himself from the creature skipping around the rooftops and waiting to find them. Their only protection was the soft continuous chant that lilted from Marion's trembling lips. Leaving her house had been hardest: she'd left her lights on so that it would not notice any change on her street and the two of them crept with tiny steps up the street, so slow that it took nearly a half hour to reach the cross street and escape the luminance. From that point onward, Jack allowed Marion to lead him through the dark, with her hand gripping his arm and squeezing it when she wanted him to slow down. When she wanted to go left, he felt himself being pulled in that direction. For a right turn, she pressed against his body and they turned. Twice, she yanked downward on his arm and the two of them stopped dead in their tracks in the middle of the street, waiting and listening until something inside Marion told her it was safe to move again. Throughout the entire trip of lefts, rights and sudden stops, the only sound that came from the pair was Marion's continuous, almost tuneful chanting.

"Ki-no-see, ki-no-wi, ki-no-waaaaaai, see-no-taaay-deeee." It was short and she continued without stopping, breathing in at the last syllable so that she would not need to take a breath in the midst of the mantra. It sounded like nonsense to Jack and he was not comforted by Marion's presence. With every step through the neighborhood, he couldn't rid his mind of the image of the creature leaping onto Marion from behind, ripping her throat out in mid-chant and then turning its horrid face on him.

It was at least an hour before Jack squinted and realized that the section of the neighborhood they were in contained no cars parked on the street: they were in the abandoned section on the outskirts of the neighborhood.

"I think we've made it," he said.

"Not yet," she answered when she'd reached the end of her mantra. "These people did make it out, thank Goodness, but for all we know..."

Jack started to pick up the pace. "We're nearly there!"

"Stay with me!" she hissed and continued chanting. They continued walking, nearly waddling, up the street. Jack wasn't certain if this was the same abandoned area that he'd entered through because of the darkness.

When they reached a four-way intersection, Marion yanked down on Jack's arm and he stopped. She reached into her coat and pulled out a flashlight. Jack felt an urge to grab it away from her, afraid that she would alert the thing to their presence, but his frozen arms never made a move. Instead, Marion turned on the flashlight and pointed it up at the street signs.

Tyler and Jones.

"Is this where you came from?"

Jack let out a huge breath. "Yes, thank you. It's just this way." He motioned to his right and tried to pull Marion with him, but she refused to budge.

"You should be safe from this point onwards," she said.

She tuned off the flashlight and Jack had to blink in the dark before he could see her face again. "Look, there's no reason for you to go back there. You can stay at my place for a while," he said.

"We don't have time for this," she said.

"I know, but..."

"I have to go back and try to find a way to stop this. It's the least I can do."

She tried to turn back but Jack grabbed her arm. "You might be able to find the answer easier if you're out here. You'll have access to libraries and..."

But Marion shook herself out of his grasp and backed up two steps. "And who will help the next one like you who comes wondering in? The rest of them are too scared. It's the least I can do!"

"Then tell me what you're looking for!" Jack was trying hard not to be loud as he rasped his words out to her.

She continued to walk backwards away from him. "Don't go looking for it. You may do more harm than good. It's the least I can do."

"But..."

Marion turned the flashlight back on him and started chanting. Knowing he could be seen, Jack ran out of the beam of light, which flicked off as soon as he was headed in the right direction. After twenty quick steps, Jack found himself on the edge of Magnolia Boulevard, now quiet with piddling, quarter-to-four traffic. The only sound he could hear above the cold air was Marion's mantra, disappearing back into the neighborhood behind him.

* * *

That was ten days ago. I tried calling the police as soon as I got home but they hung up on me. I guess I shouldn't be surprised: they must've gotten a slew of calls concerning that neighborhood before mine. Marion was right in that respect: the police had evidently decided that they'd had enough of whatever it was that was going on in that neighborhood and were determined to let nature (as if there was anything natural about what was slinking around the darkened streets) take its course. Although I didn't expect to get much headway, I felt I would be remiss if I didn't try calling the newspapers. I got the same response. As soon as I said "There's something funny going on in the residential neighborhood southeast of Magnolia and Cold...", I got a click and dial tone. No one wanted to know and everyone hoped that it would just go away.

I wrote up everything that happened to me, describing the whole thing in the third person (and using a bogus name) as if it were a story that I made up. I didn't think you'd believe me if I came up to you and told you that I'd gone wondering around a neighborhood in the middle of the night and met up with some flesh-eating monster (or whatever it was). But to say, "Here, sit down, I've got a yarn to tell you that you just won't believe": that got your attention.

I just came down from the roof of my apartment building, a place where I spend much of my time once the sun goes down. I use binoculars to look down into the neighborhood: very few of the houses keep their lights on any more. I have noticed an especially bright glow coming from close to the far end, closer to Riverside Drive than Magnolia. I can only guess that it's Marion's house and that she is still open for business: burning the midnight lights to find something in her books to send the thing away and attracting the attention of any wanderers who might be lucky enough to have made it to her doorstep without meeting up with the monster.

Sometimes, I can almost see a figure, leaping from rooftop to rooftop. The sound it makes when it howls travels on the midnight wind and makes me hunker down, afraid that it might look to the north and spot me.

The last thing I have to say is that two days after I walked out of the neighborhood, I put up my Christmas lights up on the terrace. It has nothing to do with the Christmas Spirit: I've never felt less like celebrating the holidays than I have in the last ten days. All I can think about are the lights on Marion's house, which glowed so bright and brilliantly in the night and brought me safely to her door.

Someday, maybe Marion will make it out of there. And if she does, maybe she'll see my lights and find me.

It's the least I can do.

NEW YEAR'S EVE

FADE OUT

Richard sat back from the typewriter and his hair was tingling on the back of his neck but he didn't care. If his hair had been on fire, he doubted if he would have given it a second thought. But this was a time for tingling, for excitement, for a heart to beat fast. And his heart was indeed beating fast.

Are you scared?

No, strangely enough Richard wasn't in the least scared. In fact, he was more scared that the events of the evening to come wouldn't go exactly as planned. Instead, all he could see and understand about what was going to happen seemed to be completely normal and natural, even comforting. And there was power to be felt as well: it flowed through his veins and made him smile. He even felt a familiar throb between his legs and his smile grew wider; too bad that it would go to waste like so many before it, but that didn't matter anymore. Richard Tonker looked at what he had written on his monitor (or so he guessed, as he had no memory of it) and couldn't wait to read it to Laurie. Not that she would want to hear it, but he would read it to her anyway and she would listen.

There's no doubt… she'll listen… it says so right here.

Richard hit Control-P and the thirty-four pages started printing. His craned his neck to see the pages as they came out: the print was irregular as befitted a printer that was already five years old and needed replacing. Richard felt almost embarrassed that such a document should receive its first (*Only – be fair – this is the only copy that will ever exist*) printing in such a ragged state. But it would have to do. There was no time to go down to Staples and get a new printer. It was after six o'clock on December 31st and the stores were closed… for good.

No more waiting in line to pay. No more having to replace your worn-out computer components. No more disappointing McCartney albums. No more God-awful comic-book action movies or reality shows starring Paris Hilton. No more Laurie. No more anything.

Just five hours and forty-two minutes to go.

Just thirty-four pages to go.

* * *

"Yeah, Foxfire at nine sounds good to me. We'll ring in the new year with a bang like you never heard before." Laurie was yammering on her cell phone as Richard emerged from his home office. She looked up briefly, noticed the strange look on his face, but allowed Jane's voice on the other end to push aside whatever suspicious thoughts she might have had about such a creepy smile. "What? Oh, you mean Shakespeare? No, I don't think he'd come along, even if I considered inviting him." She said this last pointedly with her eyes firmly fixed on him as he entered the room, wanting him to know. While her voice remained light as she spoke into the phone, her eyes remained fixed and stern as he came in and simply leaned against the wall and waited for her to be finished. If she'd taken a moment to think of something other than her plans for the evening with Jane, she might have considered how much she didn't like the way he stood there, smiling with his arms crossed. As usual, he had a few pages in his hand that he would no doubt soon be begging her to read.

Not tonight, she thought. Tonight is for dancing, not for glancing.

"Sounds good," she said. "I'll see you then. Happy New Year." She hung up and looked at Richard, surprised to see him looking so smug. That wasn't usual, but she knew she could match it easily and did so. "And what are you looking so satisfied for?"

Richard didn't answer. "Going out to the Foxfire tonight?"

"Yes," she said, "and you're not coming. Only fun people are invited."

"It's a public place. Anybody can walk in." He spoke without any sort of effort to push his point of view, as if he were simply reading lines from an uninteresting scene he had to play.

Laurie stood up and straightened her t-shirt. "Sure they can: anybody whose idea of fun is something other than tapping on a keyboard day and night, writing scripts that nobody's ever going to read, let alone pay for."

"Somebody will read this one," he said, his voice nearly giggling with confidence.

"Yeah? Who?"

"Well, I thought that you might find a little time to glance through it and…"

Laurie brayed a laugh. "Excuse me. Earth-to-Rich: tonight is New Year's Eve and I'm meeting Jane at the Foxfire. We're gonna dance, drink and maybe talk to someone who…"

Laurie suddenly sneezed loudly.

"Geshundheit," Richard said. "You catching cold?" Again, he spoke in a flat, uninterested voice.

"No," she sniffed. "Anyway, I was saying I might talk with someone who doesn't think that all I want to do with my life is read your scripts and wait for some producer to lose his mind long enough to cut you a check."

"You used to like my scripts."

"Yeah... well... I suppose we all liked fairy tales when we were young. But most of us grow up, Rich. Some of us realize that if the dream doesn't come true by the time they turn thirty, then it probably isn't going to. They don't cling to it like some wild dog in an alley chewing on chicken bones. Now if you'll excuse me, I'm gonna..."

"...put on my red pumps and get the hell out of here before you can trap me into being your editor," they were both saying in perfect symmetry: Laurie off the top of her head and Richard reading aloud from one of the pages in front of him. Confused, Laurie's voice faltered to a stop and Richard's trailed off with her. He shrugged and looked up from the page.

"Apparently that's all you wanted to say."

Laurie stood there and looked at Richard's smile, liking it less with every second that she was forced to remain in ignorance about what just happened. She'd seen that same look on the faces of people like David Copperfield and David Blaine after they'd looked into their audiences and confirmed that every mouth was hanging open in astonishment.

"Nice trick," she said. "How'd you do it?"

"Nice to hear that Jane's knee won't be bothering her tonight. She'll be able to dance until midnight."

Laurie's eyes closed slightly. "Have you been listening to me while I was on the phone?"

"Didn't have to," he said, waving the pages. "It's all right here."

"New pilot?"

Richard chuckled. "More of a one-off special. Take a listen." He flipped to the top page.

"I told you, I don't have time to…"

But Richard ignored her and started reading. "Interior – Tonker Living Room – Evening. Laurie, the former student and now faithless girlfriend of screenwriter Richard Tonker…"

"*Failed* screenwriter," she interjected, but Richard took no notice.

"…is sitting in the easy chair talking with her friend Jane about the New Year's Eve festivities ahead of them. LAURIE: 'I haven't eaten yet, so I'm gonna go out to Barone's and get something light and talk with Michelle for a while. She's on the bar tonight. Anything to get away from Dr. Frankenstein. He probably won't even know that I'm gone.'"

Laurie gasped angrily. "You *were* listening to me, you son-of-a…"

Richard kept going, speaking louder to drown her out. "JANE: 'Well, I have a few things to do first, so I won't be able to get to the Foxfire until nine or so, but don't worry: my knee hasn't bothered me in a few weeks and I'm ready to shake it tonight.' LAURIE: 'Yeah,

Foxfire at nine sounds good to me. We'll ring in the new year with a bang like you never heard before.' JANE: 'What about Richard? Is he coming?' LAURIE: 'What? Oh, you mean Shakespeare? No, I don't think he'd come along, even if I considered inviting him.'"

Richard continued reading from his manuscript and Laurie found herself doing something she swore she wouldn't be doing tonight of all nights: listening to him. She felt herself slowly sitting back down on the couch, certain that she was the victim of a very unfunny prank, designed by Richard to make her look stupid, and she didn't want to show him that it was working.

But he kept reading and Laurie's head starting pounding.

"Wait a minute, wait a minute," she said, waving her hands in the air. "How could you possibly know what she said to me? What, have you got some device that taps into my phone so you can hear all my conversations? I might have known that you would be the jealous, paranoid type. I just didn't realize the level that you'd sink to..."

But Richard stopped reading and held out the pages to her. "Here, I think you should read this for yourself. You've already heard the first two pages, so start on three."

"I told you wasn't going to spend the evening reading your..."

"Ah, I know you want to."

He was right; she did want to and she hated him for catching her like this. She didn't know exactly how he'd pulled it off, but he'd heard both sides of her conversation with Jane...

...*but he had those pages with him when you were still talking to her*...

...and he'd tricked her into momentarily forgetting that he was nothing more than a burned-out English professor still trying in vain to sell a script or novel. The only reason she remained in his apartment was because it was cozy and she didn't want to upset a good thing, especially when he was usually too mousey to stop her from doing whatever it was she wanted, but this was just too much. This was damn near psychotic. Free rent or not, the old year was moving on and Laurie knew that she was going to go with it just as soon as...

Richard held the pages out to her. Hating herself, she took them and flipped to page three. She began to read.

```
Richard enters the living room with some pages
and leans against the wall, smiling smugly.
Laurie fixes him with a glare and winds up her
conversation.

                    LAURIE
                 (on phone)
          I'll see you then.
          Happy New Year.

She hangs up.

                    LAURIE
          And what are you
          looking so
          satisfied for?

                    RICHARD
                 (ignoring her)
          Going out to the
          Foxfire tonight?
```

                    LAURIE
                  (bitchy)
            Yes, and you're not
            coming. Only fun
            people are invited.

                    RICHARD
            It's a public
            place. Anybody can
            walk in.

Laurie stands, straightening her T-shirt.

                    LAURIE
            Sure they can:
            anybody whose idea
            of fun is something
            other than tapping
            on a keyboard day
            and night, writing
            scripts that
            nobody's ever going
            to read, let alone
            pay for.

Laurie's breath stopped momentarily and she fought an urge to look up at Richard, imagining how he must have been staring at the top of her head as she leaned over the pages. She had no wish to see that look and the only alternative was to keep reading.

                    LAURIE
          Excuse me. Earth-
          to-Rich: tonight
          is New Year's Eve
          and I'm meeting
          Jane at the
          Foxfire. We're
          gonna dance, drink
          and maybe talk to
          someone who...

She sneezes.

                    RICHARD
          Geshundheit. You
          catching cold?

                    LAURIE
               (sniffling)
          No. Anyway, I was
          saying I might talk
          with someone who
          doesn't think that
          all I want to do
          with my life is
          read your scripts
          and wait for some
          producer to lose
          his mind long
          enough to cut you a
          check.

She had to look at him, there was no other way. She did and saw that horribly self-satisfied grin spread so wide across his face that it looked almost demonic. "What the Hell is this?"

"Well, it's the future." He sounded as if no explanation should have been necessary.

"The future? But we just said this stuff."

"True, but when I wrote it, it *was* the future. Call it a prediction, if you like. An accurate prediction, as it turned out."

Laurie continued reading.

                         RICHARD
                 You used to like my
                 scripts.

                         LAURIE
                 Yeah… well… I
                 suppose we all
                 liked fairy tales
                 when we were young.
                 But most of us grow
                 up, Rich. Some of
                 us realize that if
                 the dream doesn't
                 come true by the
                 time they turn
                 thirty, then it
                 probably isn't
                 going to. They
                 don't cling to it
                 like some wild dog
                 in an alley chewing
                 on chicken bones.
                 Now if you'll
                 excuse me, I'm
                 gonna…

Richard suddenly starts reading from the pages,
magically matching what Laurie is saying the

moment she says it.

                    RICHARD & LAURIE
                       (together)
           ... put on my red
           pumps and get the
           hell out of here
           before you can trap
           me into being your
           editor...

Laurie, surprised, trails off and Richard does
the same as he has no more lines to read.

                    RICHARD
           Apparently that's
           all you wanted to
           say.

Laurie put the bundle of pages next to her on the couch. She wanted to get up, get her red pumps on (*just like it said I said in the script – how the Hell did he know that...*) and settle her rumbling stomach with a plate of seafood salad at Barone's like she planned, but the spring in her muscles, needed to get her back on her feet and out the door, had all but gone dead inside her. She merely looked at Richard, whose smile had turned into a wild glare. He was waiting for her to say something, or maybe...

He wants me to be silent. That's how he'll know that he got to me.

"I suppose you think that I'm impressed." The steady tone she was hoping for didn't quite make it out of her mouth.

"I think you might be scared."

"I'm not scared."

"You should be."

"Well, I'm not."

"I knew you were going to say that."

"Stop it!"

"It's on page five. This whole part of the conversation is on page five. It's quite extraordinary, really. I didn't memorize my lines or anything. I'm simply talking like normal, but the entire time I can picture the words on the page; everything that you and I are saying..."

"STOP IT!" This time the spring was back in her and she was standing in front of him and shouting into his face. "I SAID, STOP IT!"

"I knew you were going to say that," he said.

The blood rushed to Laurie's face and she swung her fist at him. However, he ducked in plenty of time and it passed over his head.

"I knew you were going to do that."

"Oh yeah? Did you see this coming?" She snapped her knee up, in search on the spot between his legs that would wipe the smile off his face, but instead it connected with the hand that reached down to stop her just in time.

"Yes."

And now Laurie felt scared for the first time; after anticipating all of her blows, she briefly wondered if he could somehow hear what she was thinking.

He doesn't have to hear you; everything is written right on your face.

His smile wouldn't stop; that's what unnerved her the most. And that smile had no relation to the one that she'd found so warm and endearing whenever he'd looked over at her during his lectures and when she first toyed with the old schoolgirl fantasy of bedding her college professor.

He's snapped, she thought. And yet, somehow, he's managed to...

Laurie simply turned from him and ran for the bedroom, kicking up the lint and dust of the hardly-vacuumed carpet. She slammed the door behind her and leaned against it, fearing that he might try to break in to recite more of what she had said or, even creepier, what she was going to say soon. She forced herself to stop breathing heavily so that she could hear whether he was coming. There was no sound from the living room or hall.

After taking a moment to wait for her heart to slow down, Laurie splashed some water on her face, applied makeup, slipped into her red pumps (he knew I was going to put these on... I just bought them today... how did he know I even had them... he even knew I was going to SNEEZE, for Christ's sake!), and was ready to leave. All she had to do was open the door, which she did after taking a deep breath and holding it.

He was sitting on the couch just next to the front door. She knew there was no way he would let her out of the apartment without at least one more chance to freak her out. Laurie let the breath out, straightened her shoulders and strode down the hall to the front door. She would've been out the door if she hadn't needed to fumble for her keys in her pocketbook. That was the moment that Richard, who was looking at the last page of the script, chose to speak up.

"This can't be happening."

"What?"

"This... can't... be... happening," he enunciated.

She chuckled a bit, but without any humor. "I guess that's my line you're reading."

"Very good."

"Yeah, well... it sounded like something I would say right about now."

He looked up at her. "It's the last thing you say."

"Fine," she spat. "It will be the last thing I say to you because I'm not coming back, got it? I'll stay with Jane tonight and send my brother around to get my things. He's really big and used to be a marine so..."

While she was talking, Richard flipped to an earlier page. He started reading aloud as she spoke. "...I would advise you to stay out of his way because... STOP IT!"

They both yelled the last at the same time. Laurie bit back the urge to scream at him. Instead, she decided to give what she thought would be her departing line.

"This can't be happening." Keys in hand, she turned to the door.

"No, you misunderstood me. That's the last thing you say before midnight comes... your last words."

Her hand faltered on the way to the doorknob, her fingers tingling.

"You wanna hear it?" he asked. "It's only fair." Without waiting for a response, he flipped to the last page and began to read aloud. "Laurie backs away from Richard, mistaking the look on his face for murderous intent. She steps in the puddle of vomit and her foot slips out from under her. She falls, landing on her butt, and in this position finally takes a good look at the sky above her. The midnight sky has turned blood red and…"

Laurie's hand shot out and clutched the knob, forgetting momentarily how it worked.

"But you haven't heard the whole thing. You haven't heard your line, yet!"

She whimpered but refused to say anything to him, to be pulled into his crazy world for even one more second. She knew she would go crazy if he read her one more word.

Richard laughed as he spoke again. "Well, watch your toes tonight. And say 'Hi' to Rex for me."

Laurie had the door open and went though it with her hands over her ears, moaning to block out the sound of his voice. She ran down the hall to the stairway without closing the door behind her. Richard got up and closed it.

He sat back down and re-read the last page of the script one more time.

```
Laurie is still bent over, gasping, and doesn't
hear Richard approach until he is nearly upon
her.
```

                    RICHARD
              Did anything
              interesting happen
              tonight?

Laurie turns and is standing again, terrified.

                    LAURIE
              How did you do
              that? Was he a
              friend of yours?

                    RICHARD
              I don't know how it
              happened; it all
              just came to me. I
              was just… sure.

                    LAURIE
              This is crazy!

                    RICHARD
              You know what
              happens next, don't
              you? Remember what
              I said before you
              left home?

                    LAURIE
              Keep away from me!

Laurie backs away from Richard, mistaking the
look on his face for murderous intent. She steps
in the puddle of vomit and her foot slips out
from under her. She falls, landing on her butt,
and in this position finally takes a good look at
the sky above her. The midnight sky has turned
blood red and, after the cry of "Happy New Year"
is heard, the sound of thousands of voices

screaming can be heard in the wind, which has
suddenly started blowing in a horrific fury.

                    LAURIE
                  (screaming)
          This can't be
          happening!

Richard looks up at the sky and, seeing that his
prophesy has been fulfilled to the letter, starts
laughing. It is truly the end of the world and
he is not afraid.

                                    FADE OUT

                      * * *

"Everyone, listen up! We've got five minutes to go before midnight!"

The whole bar whooped and everyone there, with the exception of one young lady sitting at the bar, either raised their drinks high or scrambled to order one more before the hour struck. Only Laurie had resisted any urge to celebrate and instead felt a cold, ever-expanding lump in her stomach when she looked up at the clock and saw how close to midnight it was. When she left the apartment earlier in the evening, she'd hoped that getting amongst normal people (and by normal she meant anyone who wasn't a creepy writer who spent way too much time thinking up ways to scare her) and getting a few drinks down her throat might dispel the curse that Richard had endeavored to place on her. But Michelle, the bartender at Barone's whose jokes always made her laugh, had given her at least a half hour of material without raising a smile on her face. She'd asked if she was sick. Laurie had only shrugged, bypassed the menu and ordered a martini. She'd had another before leaving and hadn't felt in the least bit buzzed, despite not having eaten anything since two o'clock. She'd managed to make it to the Foxfire and had another drink before Jane turned up. Laurie had tried to join her friend in the spirit of the evening, but it was forced, artificial and whatever spirit she did exhibit came from the drinks that were finally having their affect on her. After an hour, she'd been the loudest (and most annoying, even she could see it) person in the bar. And now with just a few minutes to go before the New Year, she was drunkenly leaning on her raised fist at the bar, Jane having decided that Laurie was no fun and emigrating over to another group. Laurie shivered as she failed to keep her thoughts away from the things Richard had said to her. She'd spent the entire night trying to understand how he'd done it and the one solution she kept coming back to was unacceptable.

The music throbbed and blasted, the crowd whooped louder and Laurie took another sip of her cold gin, feeling lonelier than she ever had in her entire life.

"Hey, Pretty-Girl."

Her head lolled to the side and there was a young, handsome man leaning towards her. He probably would've looked even more handsome if the booze hadn't put such a stupid grin on his face. But she was so drunk that it actually looked charming.

"Hey, Big-Guy," she said, shouting to be heard.

"I've been looking at you all night and you just don't fit in here. Everybody else is happy and it ain't right that you're just sitting here by yourself."

Laurie smiled, having forgotten how fun it could be to be picked up. "So what are you gonna do about it?"

He looked down and laughed, trying to clear his head long enough to say the next bit without slurring. "Well, we've still got a couple of minutes on this song before the countdown. Let's dance."

Laurie tried to demur, but there wasn't any strength in her protest and she was glad when her wrists were grasped and she was pulled off the stool into the middle of the crowded floor. Neither of them had much strength to keep the beat and they fell against each other almost immediately, laughing.

"You're not too good at this, are you?"

"Just trust me, and you'll be dancing on a cloud as the clock strikes midnight," he said, trying to sound serious and failing.

"Oh, that's sweet. What's your name?"

His whiskey-stained breath hit her in the face as he said, "Rex Jones."

He leaned against her again, but this time he felt a rigid body supporting him. "What do you mean 'Rex Jones'?"

He couldn't help but laugh at her shocked face. "That's my name, Baby. And everything you've heard about me is true. Trust me."

"Did my boyfriend put you up to this?"

"What?"

"Did he tell you I would be here? Did he tell you to come over and talk to me?"

Rex was trying to clear his mind enough to figure out what he'd done to piss this pretty girl off. "Your boyfriend? Is he here now?"

Laurie placed her hands on his shoulders to steady him and make him hear her. "Listen, you must've talked with him earlier: Professor Richard Tonker from Valley College. Please tell me that this is all a gag! He set this up, right?"

Rex shook himself free of her grasp and attempted to pull her closer. "Look Baby, I don't know what you're talking about, but this song ain't gonna last much longer and I came out here to dance. Now if you'll just…"

"Ow!"

"Oh, I'm sorry."

"You stepped on my foot!"

"I'm sorry, I lost my balance. Why don't we sit down and…"

But Laurie grabbed his shoulder and looked into his eyes, hoping to see the truth she wanted there. "He told you to do that, didn't he?"

Rex was starting to lose his patience. "What are you talking about?"

"My boyfriend told you to stomp my toes, right? Because that's what he told me would happen. Damn it, tell me the truth!"

She slapped his face and realized from the immediate look of rage that he'd been innocent of everything except drunken clumsiness. His fingers curled into a fist and he hesitated just long enough to give her a chance to turn and leap through the crowd for the door. She knocked against the backs of formerly happy drunks and drinks went sloshing onto neighbors' shirts. The festive mood suddenly turned sour as everyone looked around for who had jostled them and chose the wrong man. Cheery whoops turned into hard-edged shouts and in the confusion, not even the bartender saw Laurie running for the door with one hand on her stomach.

Laurie made it outside to the parking lot and one deep breath of the cold air brought forth a cough, which in turn brought forth a choke and her stomach lurched. She limped over to the nearby dumpster and leaned over in time to see the hot rush of gin and bile shooting to the pavement. Her supporting arm shook and nearly spilled her into her own sick, but she held herself up as the last of it dripped from her mouth. Tears sprung to her eyes as she thought of the image she must've made to anyone passing by, to anyone who might be behind her at that very…

And then she remembered Richard's final scene.

"Did anything interesting happen tonight?"

Laurie turned and stood up in time to see Richard advancing on her in the parking lot. That look in his eyes from earlier was still there, but it had intensified. Professor Richard Tonker was gone, never to return, and Richard Tonker the Mad Prophet was left in his place, ready to bring down hellfire on the entire world in revenge for a life of disappointment.

And his most immediate target of revenge was young Laurie Brixton.

I can't believe it! There has to be another answer!

"How did you do that?" she asked. "Was he a friend of yours?"

Richard kept coming, talking in that flat, possessed voice. "I don't know how it happened; it all just came to me. I was just… sure."

"This is crazy!"

Maybe he agreed with her, but if he did, he certainly didn't care.

"You know what happens next, don't you? Remember what I said before you left home?"

She started backing away from him, frightened. "Keep away from me!"

Suddenly she slipped and fell; the wind was knocked out of her and the seat of her pants was sticky from her own puke. As she gasped to regain her air, she looked above her for the first time since leaving the bar.

The sky had turned blood-red and it looked as if it was falling to swallow up the Earth. The wind suddenly whipped into a force and blew her hair all around her face.

All around them, Richard and Laurie heard the screams of "Happy New Year" followed almost immediately by a different type of scream: it was the horrified sound of those who had looked up into the sky. The world was screaming and she could hear every voice with horrible clarity. She breathed in deep for what she knew would be the last time and screamed.

"THIS CAN'T BE HAPPENING!"

Richard looked up at the sky and knew it was the end, just as he saw it. He couldn't understand why he wasn't afraid, but he decided it was best not to ask that question right now. Instead, he laughed.

Fade out.

6285998R0